CASSANDRA

A LT. KATE GAZZARA NOVEL BOOK 2

BLAIR HOWARD

- **ISBN-10:** 1093471514
- **ISBN-13:** 978-1093471519

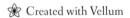 Created with Vellum

BOOKS BY BLAIR HOWARD

THE HARRY STARKE NOVELS

Harry Starke

Two for the Money

Hill House

Checkmate

Gone

Family Matters

Retribution

Calypso

Without Remorse

Calaway Jones

Emoji

Hoodwinked

Apocalypse

Aftermath

THE LT. KATE GAZZARA NOVELS

SOUTH CHICKAMAUGA CREEK, 1992

The leaves in the trees along the South Chickamauga Creek Gorge were still mostly green but soft shades of yellow and orange were starting to appear. The air was warm but there was an underlying coolness about it: the first tingles of the coming fall season.

The trail snaked through the nature preserve for miles serving hikers, bike riders, joggers, and roller-bladers. There was no shortage of people who took advantage of the area. But at that hour, just a few short minutes after dawn, all was quiet.

It was one of those morning's nature lovers cherished. After a gentle rain the previous night, a few deep breaths of the crisp, clean air alerted the senses, promising it was going to be a beautiful day.

So far, the three lady hikers traveling the path had not been disappointed.

"Did you write down the red-headed woodpecker?" Marjorie asked.

"I did, Marjorie."

"What about the goldfinch, Brenda?" Rose asked.

"*Yes*, Rose."

"There is no need to snap, *Brenda*," Rose said.

"You keep on asking me if I wrote down every bird we see even though you've watched me do it," Brenda replied, rolling her eyes. "I couldn't have been a nurse for so many years if I didn't know how to make notes."

"It's just that I don't want you to miss anything," Rose said, patting her friend of over thirty years on the shoulder. "This was a brilliant idea for a vacation, and I want to remember every bird we see."

"Shh," Marjorie interrupted, her hands splayed as she patted the air in front of her. "Look." She pointed up to a low hanging branch where an adult barred owl sat majestically preening itself.

All three women gasped. Brenda quickly made note of it. Marjorie grabbed the camera that was hanging from her neck and took aim. And they held their breaths. Only the click, click, click of the shutter disturbed the silence. Rose watched the beautiful bird through her binoculars. For several seconds it stared down at them disdainfully, obviously unconcerned, then it shook itself vigorously, spread its wings and, seemingly in slow motion, launched itself off the branch, up into the trees and disappeared from view.

"Oh, my gosh!" Rose gushed. "That alone made the entire trip worth it."

"Did you see how the feathers around his face were like the rings of a tree trunk? And those black eyes. They would be very spooky if you saw them at night," Brenda said. "Did you get some nice photos, Marjorie?"

"I did, look." She held the camera for them to see. "They should print out beautifully," she said as she started to walk further along the path. Slowly, the excitement wore off and they spoke together in hushed voices again, each looking in a different direction, taking in the scenery, searching for more birds.

Under the brush, just to the right, a quartet of gray squirrels chased each other back and forth, kicking up dead leaves and rustling the plants and saplings before darting up and around the trunks of trees.

Overhead, the early morning sun was cutting through the treetops sending shafts of golden light to the ground.

"It's as if God's shining spotlights on the beauty of His nature," Brenda whispered.

Marjorie continued to take pictures, sometimes standing directly beneath the thick, brownish-gray trunk of an old tree aiming her camera straight up. Sometimes she was focusing directly down on a spray of wildflowers.

The women belonged to The National Society of Bird-watchers Northeastern Chapter. This was their fifth trip together birdwatching in another state, and it was turning out to be the most exciting one yet. It had been Brenda's idea to add Tennessee to their list of vacation destinations. She had already filled several pages of her cataloging notebook with names and descriptions of the birds they'd seen. Rose had made quick sketches in her art journal. And Marjorie, of course, was cataloging everything on film.

"There's a little opening up ahead." Brenda pointed

with her binoculars in hand. "I think I can see water up there. I'll bet we'll see a lot of wildlife around that area."

"Good call, Bren. Ouch! I think I have a rock in my shoe." Rose wrinkled her nose as she flexed her right foot.

"There's a bench," Brenda said. "I wouldn't sit on the ground. It's still wet, and you'll get all muddy."

"I'm sure she's sat in worse," Marjorie joked.

"Oh, very funny." Rose smiled and hustled past her friends, limping slightly on her left foot.

She reached the bench and sat down, bent over to untie her hiking boot, but stopped, the boot lace in her hand, her eyes wide. She lifted her head, listening. There it was again. It was the tiniest chirp, but Rose was sure it was either a bluebird or another goldfinch. Her left foot slipped easily out of the boot, but Rose held still, unwilling to take the chance of scaring away their latest visitor.

"I think it's coming from over there." Marjorie pointed to what appeared to be a narrow dirt track through the trees. A thick carpet of wet leaves glistened darkly in the undergrowth and made it difficult to see where the concrete ended and the dirt trail began.

Bent almost double and taking careful steps, like she was performing a sobriety test, Marjorie quickly and quietly crept in the direction of the chirping, never for a moment taking her eyes from the eyepiece of her camera. She swung the camera left and right, searching for the source of the beautiful chirping sounds. Then, out of the corner of her eye she saw something else: something not beautiful at all.

She stopped, lowered her camera and stared.

"What is it, Margie?" Brenda asked as she approached. She looked in the direction of the something that now held Marjorie transfixed. At first Brenda's mind didn't register what she'd seen.

Someone dumped a mannequin in the brush, she thought. *How rude that they would litter such a beautiful part of the trail.*

"What are you looking at?" Rose asked, having replaced her hiking boot. And then she saw it too, and she gasped, and grabbed Rose's arm.

"Oh, my God... No," she whispered.

Although the other two women said nothing, they both thought the same thing. First, that it was a trick of the light, then that perhaps they were imagining things.

They felt for each other's hands, held on tightly and carefully approached what they desperately hoped wasn't what they thought it was.

"Oh, my God," Rose said again and made the sign of the cross.

"I don't believe it." Marjorie shook her head.

Brenda gasped, sucked in a huge breath, and desperately tried to hold back the vomit.

From the length of the hair and the dirty pink shirt they guessed that it was the body of a female. The face was concealed, hidden behind a gray, pasty arm and thick black mud.

"Oh, my God," Rose said again. "We've got to get help."

"You two go. I'll stay here with her," Brenda said. Still the nurse even though she was long retired. "You're both faster than me anyway."

"No. You and I will stay," Marjorie said, almost in a whisper. "Rose. You go on back down the path and find a phone."

"Right... right... yes, I'll go," Rose replied and quickly walked away, back the way they had come.

"If only we were twenty years younger," Brenda said as she watched Rose hurry out of sight then turned again to the nightmare. "Should we get her out of there?"

"I don't think we should touch anything," Marjorie said.

"What if she's still alive?"

"I doubt it," Marjorie shivered. "I'll see if there is a pulse." Carefully, she stepped forward onto the dirt and mud under the low hanging trees. She hadn't gone but a few steps when she changed her mind and turned back.

"What is it?" Brenda asked. "What do you see?"

Marjorie hurried back to Brenda's side and quickly took her hand. Brenda could feel her friend's entire body trembling.

"What is it, Margie?"

"She's dead."

"You're sure?" Brenda didn't look at the body. She didn't want to see anymore.

"Yes, I'm sure. I think she's been stabbed."

Rose finally made it to the parking lot. But there was no one there, no cars, no traffic on the road. She looked desperately around, saw what she thought might be the driveway to a house, and ran toward it.

The small frame house was set back some fifty yards from the road and by the time she reached the front door, she was gasping for breath. She hammered on the door until finally an old man still in his pajamas opened it and asked her what the hell she wanted.

Breathlessly, she told him.

The police dispatcher told her to go back to the parking lot and wait. The first cruiser arrived some twenty minutes later by which time she was in a state of almost total collapse, and she still had to guide them back along the trail to where her friends were anxiously waiting, wondering what had happened to her.

To Brenda and Marjorie, it felt as if they'd been with the body for the entire morning. By the time Rose returned with the police, Brenda was near hysterics and Marjorie had to remain seated on the nearby bench. Rose was in shock and retold their movements up until they found the body as if she were reciting a grocery list.

It was to be their last bird-watching trip.

By the time Police Lieutenant Linus Peete arrived on the scene, the entire area had been quarantined behind yellow police tape. Peete had moved to Chattanooga more than ten years ago. He'd left Chicago to get away from scenes like this. True, Chattanooga had its fair share of homicides, but nothing on the scale of Chicago's South Side. So for the most part, it had been a wise move. But this one was different; it brought it all back to him. This was reminiscent of that murderous snake that slithered through the dark streets of Chicago's South Side.

"The rain hasn't done us any favors," he heard one of the officers say.

"Nope. And those three poor old girls who found the body weren't much help either. Out-of-towners. Useless," the other replied.

Peete nodded to the officers as he approached. They instinctively straightened their posture and nodded back.

"You ready, Lieutenant? Should we turn her over?" Officer Ray Morris asked. He was a good policeman: by the book and stoic. Peete knew he could count on Ray to do his job. But even he, seasoned officer that he was, couldn't hide his shaking hands.

"Did we get photos yet?" Peete muttered.

"Yeah," Ray replied.

"Hey, Lieutenant." Trey Hennessy was the crime scene photographer. He would be at the high school next week, moonlighting, taking pictures of the kids at some homecoming dance. But for now, he'd finished snapping away at the Jane Doe.

"Yep?" Peete said. "You finished..." He paused, then pointed and said, "Trey? What's that? Looks like there's a purse hanging on that tree over there." He pointed to a reddish leaved shrub. "What the hell's it doing there? Looks like someone hung it there. Did you get some shots of it?"

"Yes, sir," Trey replied.

"Okay, Ray," Peete, said, over his shoulder, still staring up into the tree. "That is a no, don't turn her over, not yet." Then he turned again to Trey, slowly walked over to the tree, stood for a minute staring up at the purse. *Yeah,* he thought. *Looks expensive. Someone hung it there, so we could see. Whoever it was, wanted us to find it. Son of a bitch... The killer?*

He took a pair of latex gloves from his pocket and pulled them on. Carefully, he lifted the purse down from the branch, opened it, and got lucky: there was a wallet inside it with a Tennessee driver's license in the clear plastic window. Jane wasn't a Doe after all.

"Oh God!" Ray gasped.

Peete looked up and saw the officer stomp away from the scene. Trey had his hand to his mouth, his eyes wide, staring.

Damn it, Peete thought, angrily. *I told him not to move her.*

"What?" he shouted.

Ray didn't answer. He was too busy throwing up.

With a horrible feeling that his stomach was about to fall out of his ass, Peete, still holding the purse, walked back to look at the body. Even he wasn't prepared for what he saw.

"Jesus, Mary and Joseph." He stared down at the body, swallowed hard, his emotions in a whirl: first nausea, then sadness, and finally anger. The body was that of a young woman in her late teens. Her head, neck, arms and chest were covered with blood mixed with thick black mud... and wounds, so many he couldn't count them.

The bastard didn't just stab her, Peete thought, *he mutilated her. He had to have been in one hell of a rage... Someone's daughter, sister, mother, maybe?*

The scene was quiet, almost ethereal. Now that the body had been discovered even the birds were showing respect. Only the occasional harsh caw of a blue-jay off in the distance disturbed the silence.

Dr. Richard Sheddon had been Hamilton County's chief medical examiner for just three months when he arrived at the scene on South Chickamauga Creek some thirty minutes after Peete. He was a small man in his early thirties, five-eight, a few pounds overweight, his hair already receding, with a round face that usually sported a jovial expression, but not today. He clicked his tongue and shook his head when he saw the body.

"Hey, Linus," he said, dumping his big black bag on the ground, jerking Peete out of his trance. "What do we have here? I wish you hadn't moved her."

"Yeah, me too," Peete replied, regretfully. "Her name is Cassandra Smart, nineteen. Looks like she's a student at Chattanooga State." He looked off in the direction of the University, then back down at the photo on the school ID. "What a shame. She was a pretty kid, though you wouldn't know it now, see?" He held out the ID for Sheddon to look at. Sheddon nodded. The face was framed by waves of long blonde hair and had a deep dimple in each cheek.

Peete continued to study the photo as the ME made his preliminary observations before waving for the EMTs to move the body.

The three women who'd found the body had already given their statements. They were indeed tourists, and Peete couldn't help but wonder if their first visit to Tennessee would be their last.

They'll probably avoid all nature preserves from now on, he thought, shaking his head.

"What do you make of it, Doc?" Peete asked.

"The poor kid must have really pissed someone off.

Multiple stab wounds... Dozens. God only knows what else. Her clothes and underwear appear to be intact. I can't be sure until I get her under the lights but at first glance, she doesn't seem to have been sexually assaulted."

"Thank God for that," Peete muttered. "That might be the only bit of good news, that she wasn't raped."

"She hasn't been here very long," Sheddon said. "From the state of rigor, and the liver temp, I'd say no more than eight hours... Time of death? Sometime between ten last night and one this morning I should say, but don't hold me to it. I'll give you a more accurate estimate when I've completed the postmortem."

Peete looked around the area.

I thought I was done with this kind of crap. Why can't I ever seem to catch a break... just one sweet, perfectly clear footprint, Peete wondered. *Maybe the perp dropped his wallet or car keys? He must have been batshit crazy, which means he was sloppy, too, right? So where's his mistake, then? Where is it? Where's the clue that'll lead me right to his frickin' front door? It's gotta be here somewhere, Linus. Just be patient. She'll tell you. Just give her time. Patient, my ass. If it happens, it'll be a first.*

He looked sadly at the pale face as they zipped her into the body bag. He shook his head, angrily, then turned to the two officers and had them secure and guard the scene, radioed for the CSI team, had a quick word with the three women, thanked them for their help, and then followed Doc Sheddon to his car.

"I'll do the post first thing tomorrow," Sheddon said through the open car window. "I'll expect you at nine o'clock sharp."

"I'll be there," Peete said, "unfortunately," he added, quietly, to himself. "Right now, I should go see the parents... What the hell am I going to say to them?"

Sheddon shook his head and said, "Better you than me, Linus, better you than me," and he rolled up the window and drove away leaving Peete staring absently after him.

NOVEMBER 2015

Yes, I was hiding that November morning back in 2015. It was too damn early for me to interact with anyone. I'd already gotten an idea it was going to be a bad day when I arrived at Dunkin Donuts and realized I'd forgotten my wallet. It wouldn't look good for me, a police lieutenant, to be caught driving without my license, so I turned around, went back home, and grabbed my wallet; it was sitting right there on the kitchen table next to the bottle of wine I'd cracked open the night before. By the time I got back on the road, I knew I was going to be late to work. Worse than that, I was going to have to drink the coffee from the bullpen.

My name is Lieutenant Catherine Gazzara, Kate to my friends, and back then I was a homicide detective assigned to the Major Crimes Unit along with my partner Lonnie Guest. Actually, I don't have time for friends. Just about everyone calls me Kate, including the man I was currently hiding from, Assistant Chief Henry Finkle, known to one and all as "Tiny," on account of his diminutive stature.

"Kate?" Finkle's voice grated like fingernails on a chalkboard. "You know, if you wanted to get me alone all you had to do was say so," he said as he strolled through the wire gate that separated the "morgue" from the evidence room.

"Hey, Henry. You wearing lifts? You look taller," I said, barely looking up from the folder I'd grabbed to bury my head in when I heard him coming. The morgue was not actually a morgue. It was a sad, cold and dismal room in the basement of the police department where the cold case files were stored. There were hundreds of them.

I'd had a little luck with one or two of them and, although there weren't any extra awards or pay for wrapping them up, I did feel kinda proud of myself. Finkle was there to make sure that I didn't stay proud for too long.

"You trying to come on to me, Lieutenant?" he smirked. He was a half-pint at a hair over five-foot-eight and, sad to say that when water gain was entered into the equation, I was sure I outweighed him by at least ten pounds.

"No, not hardly." I stared at the file. Cassandra Smart was the name of the dead girl. I didn't really want to add another case to my plate. I already had several still open on my desk. Several? Who was I kidding? I had enough work piled up on my desk to keep me busy for six months. But, a lot of my job was hurry up and wait. And most of my cases *had* been waiting, some of them for a long time, hence my visit to the morgue that day in the hopes I might find something... an easy DNA case I could wrap up quickly and hand the chief a positive result while I waited.

"What's that you're holding?" he asked.

I glanced down at the file and was about to give him a smart answer, but I thought better of it.

"It's a cold case file. Cassandra Smart."

"I see..." He paused, seemed distracted, stared vacantly at the file for a moment, obviously thinking about what he was going to say next.

"I thought I made it very clear yesterday evening, Lieutenant, that I needed to speak with you."

He'd obviously gotten tired of harassing me and had shifted gears.

"As you well know, we have a situation—you have a situation—that isn't going to go away. Do I need to remind you about Mrs. Shania Bolton, and of what she's accusing you?"

"Come off it, Henry," I said, resignedly. "Someone gets accused of police brutality at least three times a week in every police station across the country." Had it been anyone but Henry Finkle talking to me I would have been all "yes, sir" and "no, sir." But this was *Henry Finkle*, and he'd been looking for a reason, even a false one like Shania Bolton, to either get me tossed off the force or demoted to pencil pusher, destined to live out the rest of my career behind a desk. Well, maybe, maybe not. Maybe he was just looking for a way to pressure me into his bed.

Chief Johnston was aware of the situation and told me not to worry until there was a reason to worry. So far, that reason hadn't come up. But Finkle didn't care. He knew he could keep me off balance just enough so maybe, just maybe, I'd make a mistake that couldn't be fixed.

"I'm glad you don't feel concerned about it," he said, sarcastically. "Mrs. Bolton feels so unconcerned that she's lawyered up. John Patton."

"John Patton?" I laughed out loud. "No shit? Of course she hired him. He's a frickin' shark, with a reputation to match."

Actually, John Patton didn't like cops and had a reputation of digging deep, very deep, to find anything he could to tarnish a cop's reputation in front of a jury. Drinking a beer at a bachelor party? Laughing at an off-color joke? Wearing a bathing suit at a pool? Those innocent adventures would be turned into scandals so big it would make the O.J. Simpson trial look like a preschool lesson.

"Great, Kate. I'm glad you're not worried, about yourself, at least. But you should be concerned about how your... transgressions might tarnish the image of this department."

Transgressions? "Are you serious? Is this what you needed to tell me, Henry? That I'm not worrying enough?" I know I wasn't making the situation any better, but there was something about Finkle that forced me to be as difficult as possible.

He took a step toward me. I backed away. But it was obvious I'd overstepped my bounds.

"Be very careful, Lieutenant. You just might need a friend at a time like this." He sneered. "It's not smart to bite the hand that feeds you."

I took a deep breath and slumped. My body temperature ignited as my cheeks flushed in embarrassment. Of course I was concerned about being accused of police brutality. But usually there was a circling of the wagons. We were the thin blue line and were supposed to offer each other support when things like this happened. But Finkle was determined to let me know that as far as he was concerned, I was on my own this time.

"I want a status report on that file you have in your hand," he snapped at me, "and everything else you have on your desk... by five o'clock this afternoon, *sharp*. You need to keep your nose clean, Kate. Otherwise, I'll have no choice but to inform the Chief that due to the pressures of the investigation, you aren't able to properly handle your responsibilities, and that a temporary leave of absence might be necessary."

I'd heard of people seeing red but never really believed it. Not until that very minute. I wanted to smack the silly SOB's face, hard. Fortunately, though, before I could say anything else to get myself further in trouble, he spun on his heel and walked out of the morgue. The jerk didn't even realize he'd just assigned me a new case. Cassandra Smart and I were going to have to get to know each other, and fast.

I gave Finkle enough time to get upstairs to his own office before I left. The last thing I wanted was to get caught alone with him in the stairwell or elevator. So, like a teenager sneaking into their bedroom after curfew, I walked quickly in the direction of my office, tapping my partner Lonnie on the shoulder as I passed his cubicle.

Sergeant Lonnie Guest followed me into my office,

and I gestured for him to close the door as I sat down behind my desk.

"Where were you?" he asked. "I saw you pull up out front but then you never came in..."

"I was in the morgue. We've got a new one. Cassandra Smart." I tossed the file onto my desk, not interested in discussing it. I needed a pallet cleanser. Henry Finkle left a bad taste in my mouth.

"Hey," I said, "before we get started, what's the latest number?"

It was nice to see my partner blush and smile. Lonnie was a big boy. I mean, really big and quickly approaching that stereotypical fat cop at the donut shop we all know. Now, after having a lap band fitted, not so much.

"Eighty-eight pounds," he said bashfully.

"Eight-eight pounds in seven months? Lonnie, I am so proud of you. How are you feeling?" I asked. Anything to steer myself away from the files on the desk in front of me. Yeah, I knew I had to get the work done but right then... well, I just couldn't focus.

"I'm feeling pretty... great." He smiled. Lonnie never was a bad-looking fellow. But it was obvious that he was still lacking self-confidence. "How about you? You look like you've got a lot on your mind."

"Just business as usual." I shook my head. "I got a new case here and Finkle wants a status report by five. Would you mind—"

"Coffee?"

"Please. I didn't get any this morning."

I picked up Cassandra Smart and opened the file.

"When you get back," I said, "we'll have to hit this

and hit it hard."

"Sure, boss. I'll be back in a jiffy."

He left, closed the door behind him, and again I stared at the files on my desk, and I shuddered. *What the hell is wrong with me?*

I knew there were a few I could slap a Band-Aid on and kick down the road a few paces to keep Finkle off my back, but the rest... They would require a little more work, especially Cassandra Smart.

I stood up, walked to my window and looked outside. It was a beautiful day. If there was going to be any chance of my enjoying any of it, I was going to have to buckle down and get to work. So I did.

By the time Lonnie got back from Starbucks with my coffee, I could feel the beginnings of a migraine. I had, however, managed to plow through a couple of the files and was beginning to feel that I might have a chance, a small one, of having the reports done by five after all, but I was forgetting the new one.

"You want a donut?" Lonnie asked, holding up a small bag. I had a vision of myself demoted to a desk job gobbling down pastries. *Uggg!* I shook my head and took a sip of the hot coffee. *Better!*

"Okay, are you ready?" I asked.

Lonnie took a seat in front of my desk. I took Cassandra Smart's file and started to read. When I'd had it in my hands as Finkle was prattling on I didn't really pay it a whole lot of attention. But now that she was right in front of me, I felt a shard of guilt poke me in the gut. *This kid has been waiting for me for a long time.*

"You want to make notes?" I asked. He already had

his notebook at the ready. He nodded, and I began to read.

"Saturday morning, November 14, 1992. Three hikers, birdwatchers, stumbled on the body of Cassandra Smart on the South Chickamauga Creek Greenway trail." I took another sip of coffee.

"Cassandra was nineteen years old... Geez, she'd been stabbed forty-four times... and, according to the ME..." I checked the autopsy report and was surprised to learn who the ME was. "That would be Doc Sheddon. Wow, I knew he'd been running the department for years; this had to be one of his first cases... Anyway, according to him only seven of the forty-four stab wounds would have been fatal... Damn, Lonnie, she could have been alive for most of them. Geez, I go running on the Greenway sometimes. Doc also said that the assailant was left-handed. Well, that narrows it down a bit, I suppose."

"Crime of passion?" Lonnie asked. It was more a statement than question.

"Forty-four stab wounds? I should say so," I said as I continued to read. "The three women who found the body were tourists and all over the age of sixty, so we can cross them off the list. She, Cassandra, was a student at Chattanooga State. GPA 4.0, so she was no dummy, at least where school was concerned. Maybe not too street smart, though... Hell, who knows?" I mused.

"Boyfriend?" Lonnie asked.

"Yeah, a Mark Smirin. He would be the obvious suspect, but *obviously* they couldn't pin it on him at the time."

I flipped through the rest of the file. There were a lot of photographs of the victim... *Pretty girl,* I thought. *What the hell did she do to piss someone off so badly they stabbed her forty-four times, I wonder? Same old same old, I bet: jealousy, sex, revenge... Hmm, a Lieutenant Linus Peete was the investigating officer. I wonder if he's still around. With my luck, he'll be long dead. Worth checking, though.*

"Make a note, Lonnie. See if Lieutenant Linus Peete is still with us."

The statements from the three tourists who discovered the body were long and kind of rambling, but I could hardly blame them. They'd come from their home in Wisconsin to watch some birds and look what happened to them.

"What are you thinking?" Lonnie asked.

"I'd like to talk to Peete first, if he's still around. I've never heard of him, so he was before my time." I thought for a minute, then said, "The girl lived with her mother in Highland Park. Check to see if she still lives there. I'm thinking we might as well start with her. Go check on Peete for me, will you, please?"

He called me ten minutes later and informed me that Peete had retired in 2001 and was living in Key Largo, Florida.

Damn it. I can't justify that trip. Oh well. I guess I'll have to call him.

I checked the time. It was just after ten, so I set Cassandra aside, wrote up three more files, and then I had to get out of there, away from my desk. My head was killing me.

3

Highland Park wasn't the classiest part of town, not by a long shot, but it had improved a lot since the time of Cassandra's demise.

"What's the address again?" I mumbled, more to myself than Lonnie who was riding shotgun.

"You're looking for 312 Locust. I remember doing a bust down here when I was a rookie."

"Just one?"

"Yeah, right? A woman called in that her live-in boyfriend was beating the shit out of her, only it was the other way around."

"I'm sure there was no alcohol or drugs involved." My headache was souring my mood.

"Maybe this much." Lonnie held up his thumb and forefinger indicating a small amount. "When we got there the guy looked like he'd been attacked by a flock of birds. His face and back were all scratched."

Lonnie chuckled. I was really only half listening, wishing I could just go home, pour a glass of wine, crawl into bed and stay there until the headache passed.

"It was the scratches on his back that got him the scratches on his face." Lonnie shook his head. "His other girlfriend at the other end of the Park had long fingernails."

"Yikes." I sighed.

"Well, you know what they say, 'Don't shit on your own doorstep'... I think Locust is the next street. You think anyone will be home?"

"I'd say so. I get the feeling that there aren't too many people working nine-to-fives around here," I muttered as I observed several people loitering on porches and leaning against random cars on the street, most of them men.

The house at 312 Locust, a single-story Craftsman built in the 1930s, was set back from the street some forty feet or so and was exactly what I'd expected. It could have been a cute place except for the security bars on the windows, the patch of weeds where a lawn should have been, and the ten-foot wide stretch of broken asphalt that was the driveway.

I parked the unmarked cruiser on the street and instantly became the center of attention of the men I'd seen as we drove in. They obviously knew we were cops. I ignored them.

When I opened my car door, I heard music coming from an open window at the front of the house. It was that thud-thud-thud of bass. It poked at my head mercilessly.

Lonnie walked ahead of me and pounded loudly on the front door then stepped back, his hand on his weapon. *Geez, Lonnie. It's an old woman, not a frickin' drug dealer... I hope.*

Whoever was inside turned the music down quickly and I heard footsteps pounding back and forth.

"They're doing a little quick housekeeping for us," I said under my breath.

Lonnie nodded and cleared his throat. Finally, we heard several locks and a chain being unfastened, and the door cracked open a little.

"Peggy Smart?" I asked holding up my badge.

"Who wants to know?" The woman was a natural blonde, but her hair was graying at the temples. Her eyebrows were darker having been lined with make-up probably the night before. Black mascara was smudged around her eyes.

"I'm Lieutenant Gazzara, Chattanooga PD. This is Sergeant Guest. I'd like to talk to you about your daughter."

"What has she done now?" the woman asked as she pulled the door open a little further. She was wearing cutoff jeans and a short-sleeved button-down shirt that was buttoned crooked, the top button hole was over the second button. It was a tiny faux pas, but it was going to distract me throughout the interview. She wasn't wearing a bra either. *Gross!*

"You are Cassandra Smart's mother?" I asked.

The woman looked shocked, as if she hadn't been called that in a long time and, from the grimace she made, it looked like she'd preferred it that way. Slowly, she pulled the door open and held it for us to enter.

The home was about what I'd expected: the smell of

cigarette smoke hung heavy in the air, the furniture old and outdated on a shag rug spotted with stains that I guessed were wine or maybe coffee. There were bookshelves on either side of the fireplace, but no books just a single photograph of a pretty girl who was maybe in high school but no older; it wasn't Cassandra

"I thought you were talking about my other daughter, Tyler," she said. "Cassie was murdered back in 1992. They never caught... Oh, I see. Let me guess. You got another one. Someone else got killed, like her and now you people are forced to look into it again?"

She folded her arms across her chest. "Who is it? Some damn snob? The mayor's kid? Some frickin' doctor's kid from up on Lookout Mountain maybe? Cause Lord knows you people didn't do shit for me."

"No. I've been assigned Cassandra's case to take a second look at it," I replied.

"After all these years?" She scoffed nervously. "Good luck with that."

She tugged at her hair, rubbed her arms and shifted from her right foot to her left. She was either high or itching to get high. *Methhead?*

"You have another daughter? Tyler you said?"

"She doesn't live here anymore. Moved out when she was seventeen. I told her that was the last time I'd be posting bail and I meant it. If she's in any trouble, she'll just have to face the music. I ain't got the money or the energy to help her no more."

We stood in her living room just looking at her, waiting for her to ask us to sit. She stared back at us as if we'd just tracked mud all over her freshly mopped floor.

Finally, she shook her head and gave in, let her hands fall to her sides in defeat and offered us a seat on her couch. I sat. Lonnie remained standing. Peggy Smart sat down in an old easy chair across from me.

"Can we get on with it, Lieutenant? I don't have all day."

"You'll give us all the time we need, Ms. Smart," Lonnie interrupted.

I gifted him a sharp look that I hoped would tell him to back off a little. The woman looked skittish and I didn't want him scaring her off before I heard her story.

"If you don't mind, Ms. Smart, I'd like to record our conversation." I took out my iPad and turned on the Dictaphone voice recorder app. "It's for your benefit as much as mine... My memory isn't what it was. What can you tell me about the night Cassandra died?"

She looked at the iPad, cleared her throat, focusing her eyes on me. She had gray eyes; the tired eyes of someone who had been around the block more than a couple times. There was no need to tip-toe around the details with this one.

"It was no different from any other night," she said, looking down at her hands. "She gave me some kind of smart-ass remark about where she was going and what she was doing and that was the last I saw of her." She paused, stared at me as if waiting for me to react.

"Where was she going? What was she going to do?" I asked.

"I don't know. Like I said, she was a smartass, gave me a smartass remark and left. Didn't even tell me goodbye..."

She almost looked sad.

"You guys didn't get along?" I asked.

"No. Not really... Oh I don't know." She half-chuckled as she leaned back in her chair. "Sometimes I wonder if someone didn't switch babies with my real kid in the hospital. Cassie was just..."

"Just what?"

She shook her head and sighed. "She wasn't a slut, not really... She just couldn't say no to the boys." Peggy bit her lower lip. "Ever since she got her first training bra at the age of ten..."

I waited for her to continue. She didn't, so I said, "I understand she had a steady boyfriend." I looked at Lonnie who referred to his notebook. But before he could rattle off a name, Peggy started to laugh, bitterly.

"Just one?" The question was rhetorical. "If it had a penis you can bet she was nearby." She picked at the fabric of her armchair. "Or so everyone told me."

"Everyone? Like who?"

"Like Reginald Olley," she replied without looking at me, the hurt plain on her face. As much as I felt like avoiding what she was insinuating, I had to continue on this line of questioning.

"Reginald Olley. The man who was living with you at the time of Cassandra's death?" I cleared my throat. "Do you believe they were having an affair?"

"Look, I told the police everything I knew back in 1992. It should all be in a file somewhere," she snapped still picking nervously at the armchair fabric.

I stared at her, thinking that Cassandra had probably

been the spitting image of Peggy Smart when she was younger.

"I understand that, Ms. Smart. But sometimes time gives us a clearer perspective. Was Reginald Olley having an affair with your daughter?" The words tasted bitter in my mouth. I looked at Lonnie out of the corner of my eye. He'd been surveying the room, making mental notes of what he was seeing, but he'd stopped doing that and was looking at Peggy with interest.

"I don't have proof." Peggy bit her lip again. "But I know how he looked at her. You've seen that look, Lieutenant; I know you have. Like a frickin' wolf."

Oh yes, I'd seen it.

"Did your daughter ever say anything to you about Mr. Olley looking at her, or touching her? Did she ever complain about him?" I asked.

"She complained all the time. She complained about him, about the boys at school, about this house, about having homework, and about having to live like this." Peggy tried to stay hardened but there was a crack in the foundation. "She was never happy. Maybe she's happy now."

Suddenly, she got up from the armchair and stomped toward the front door, yanked it open, and stood there looking at the floor. I took up my iPad, shut off the recording app and stood up.

"Ms. Smart, I'm sorry if we've upset you. It's been a long time, I know... Look, if you think of anything else that might be helpful, something you might have forgotten, please give me a call. I'm going to get him."

I took a business card from my pocket and held it out

to her, but she looked out the door and said nothing, and I understood. The tears in her eyes said it all.

I set the business card on a small table by the door next to an ashtray. She'd be sure to see it eventually. Maybe she'd tear it up and leave it in the ashtray. Or maybe while she was having a cigarette, she'd remember something useful. I wasn't banking on it, but hope was sometimes all there was.

Before Lonnie and I could pull out of the driveway, she came out, running, her feet bare, across the sharp, crumbling asphalt.

I rolled my window down.

"I tossed Reggie out because he said my daughter got what she deserved," she said angrily. "He was drunk when he said it." She swallowed hard. "I don't know why the son of a bitch'd say it if he didn't... I've always thought he had something to do with it. There, now you know."

"Do you have his current address?" I asked.

She shook her head. I nodded, thanked her, told her I'd be in touch, then put the car in drive and left her standing there, her arms folded tightly across her chest, staring after us.

It was almost noon. My head was killing me. The sun seemed like it was a thousand times bigger and brighter than it had been yesterday. I headed back to the police department.

"You want me to run Reginald Olley to see if we can't get a current residence?" Lonnie asked.

"Yeah." I squinted through the windshield. "Take your time. I've got stuff I need to do back at the office and I've got to take something for my head. I don't know if it was the smoke or heaven knows what other poisonous crap was wafting through that house, but my head's ready to split."

"Can you take the afternoon off? I'll cover for you," Lonnie offered.

"With Finkle on the warpath? I don't think so... No. I'm going to barricade myself in my office and try to finish those frickin' reports."

I dreaded the idea but it had to be done. Once inside my office I pulled the blinds and made the room as dark as possible. This was one of those migraines that was going to prevent any real work from getting done. The computer screen glowed viciously. The phone rang with a horribly piercing noise that shot through my ears all the way to my spinal cord.

When five o'clock finally rolled around, I slipped from my office with my reports and updates written and went to Finkle's office.

Please be gone already. Please be gone already.

"I was about to send for you, Gazzara." He looked at his watch. "Five after five. I guess that will do."

"Here are your reports, Henry." I sighed.

"Hmm," he nodded. "Put them down. Have a seat." He motioned for me to sit down.

Oh hell. I don't need this.

"Why? What for?" I asked as I put the small stack of files on the desk in front of him.

"So that we can go over these," he said.

That was a new one. He stared at me. I was reminded of a shark that smelled blood and was circling before it struck the poor, struggling fish.

"That's not protocol," I said, quietly. "If it was, you'd have a line of guys a mile long outside the office at all times, and I wouldn't have to pull files from the morgue because your men would have done it right the first time." I didn't know where it was all coming from but I was angry; I couldn't stop myself.

"You should remember who you are talking to, Lieutenant."

I rolled my eyes. It wasn't a smart move but I was feeling bad and getting worse by the minute.

"If you weren't getting complaints from citizens for your lack of professionalism, I wouldn't have to go over your files like a fifth grader turning in her homework." He was enjoying this. Not only was my job at stake with this bogus brutality claim but now he'd also have me for insubordination.

"Fine," I muttered and took my seat. "Would you happen to have some aspirin? I've got a doozy of a headache."

"That time of the month, is it?"

I scowled at him. "What kind of damn question is that?"

He grinned at me, and said, "Fine. I know how women can be when that's an issue. I can expect very little real work to be done for the next five to seven days, right?" He snickered.

"You're way off base, Henry. I have a migraine. It's that simple." Not that it mattered to Finkle.

"Well," he said. "I've got the Chief breathing down my neck asking where you are on your files and I'll be damned if I'm going to get an ass-chewing on your account. So, go throw some cold water on your face or whatever you need to do and then we'll get started."

"I'm fine," I lied.

But it got Finkle moving. Of course, watching him move was like watching paint dry in slow motion. I watched his eyes scan through each file knowing full well which ones were closed, why the others were still open, and where I was in the process of getting things wrapped up. By the time I walked out of his office, it was ten after six and my head felt like it was going to explode. My neck was stiff and my eyes burned. Never was I so glad to get out of there and go home.

Fifteen minutes later I slammed my apartment door behind me, locked it, leaned my back against it, closed my eyes, and took several deep breaths, trying desperately to relax. I set my phone to vibrate, poured a full glass of red wine and washed down three aspirins with one gulp. Then I pulled all of the curtains plunging the entire apartment into darkness, pulled off my clothes, fell naked onto the bed and lay still, reveling in the darkness and the silence. I must have gone out like a light because I remember nothing more until I woke up at two in the morning freezing cold. Earlier that morning, I'd set the temperature to sixty-six and had forgotten to reset it.

Fortunately, though, my headache was but a faint mist of what it had been. But now I felt a slight scratching at the back of my throat.

Nope. I don't have time for a cold. Not now.

I grabbed my still almost-full glass of wine from the nightstand and picked up my phone. Lonnie, the sweet-heart, had texted me the info on Reginald Olley. The man, so it seemed, was a real Prince Charming. A lady's man for sure. I couldn't wait to meet him.

With three big gulps I finished my wine and went back to bed. Lonnie and I would be heading to East Lake first thing in the morning. Another police-friendly area. Reggie, I was sure, would be a wonderfully accommodating individual.

4

———

"How's your headache, LT?" Lonnie asked as soon as he appeared in my office bearing two cups of McDonald's coffee.

"Better. But now I have a sore throat. No cream, no sugar, right?" I asked.

"That's right. Nice and bitter." He smirked as he took a seat.

The coffee was good, and we sat quietly for several minutes enjoying the moment.

"So," Lonnie said, finally, "what's the plan?"

"I'm thinking that it might be a nice day to visit East Lake."

"East Lake? How can I resist?" he said, dryly, and I knew exactly what he meant.

It was another of those low income, high crime neighborhoods where every other home is a rental. Second and third generation families stubbornly try to hang onto and live in homes that were once majestic, and from the outside, still retain some of their old-world charm. Unfortunately, it's all an illusion. A walk to the corner convenience store after dark is something even I wouldn't risk.

When we pulled up in front of Reginald Olley's last known address, I was expecting some old dude to answer the door in boxers and with a microphone to his throat only too happy to tell us that Reggie didn't live there anymore.

But I was wrong. Lonnie stood back while I knocked on the door. Reggie was a couple of years younger than Peggy Smart, but he looked a lot older. Something you learn quickly on the job is that you don't ever judge a book by its cover.

He was wearing a stained Titans T-shirt and blue jeans, bare-foot, thin from smoking and drinking the majority of his meals, but he had muscles. Guys like him worked construction jobs all their lives, were paid under the table in cash so long as they showed up and did as they were told and didn't try to steal the copper wire and piping or tools. He was the quintessential bar room tough guy, or so he thought. I'd met and arrested a hundred more just like him.

"Good morning." I cleared my throat as I held up my badge. "Mr. Reginald Olley?"

"I've been home all night," he snarled. "My mother and my fiancée can vouch for me." He folded his arms across his chest and leaned against the doorframe. His graying hair, uneven and blocky in places, looked as if he'd cut it himself. His cheeks were sunken making his cheekbones and eyes protrude. There were crude prison tattoos on his forearms that I couldn't read. They were probably the names of children he'd had and maybe even loved. Loved enough to walk away from them. Loved enough to behave in prison until he was paroled.

"Nobody cares what your mother or your fiancée can vouch for," Lonnie said. "We want to talk to you about Cassandra Smart."

Reginald's eyes glazed over for a moment and a sick smirk crossed his lips. "You've got to be kiddin' me. Okay, let me guess. Peggy sent you over here," he said nodding.

"She suggested we talk to you, yes," I replied. "May we come in?"

He narrowed his eyes as he looked first at Lonnie and then at me. Even though the guy was at least a decade older than us, I was sure that, in a brawl, he'd not only hold his own but take a few good ol' boys down with him. He didn't budge.

"Mr. Olley, we can talk here in the comfort of your own home or we can take you down to headquarters. It's up to you," I said, smirking right back at him.

Finally, as if he really had a choice, he turned and walked into the house, leaving the door open behind him. Lonnie and I followed.

The house was simple on the inside, smelled like stale cigarettes and moth balls, and I was pretty sure that I detected a hint of marijuana. But even if I wanted to bust him on it, I'd get that worn-out old song and dance about it being medicinal.

As far as I could tell, the curtains hadn't been parted since the Carter administration. The furniture was old, worn and bald in patches from the same asses sitting in them the same way for years. I noticed crazy knick-knacks only an older person might collect and display. Teacups and porcelain kittens and a couple of faded pictures. One looked like Olley when he was a teenager. In the other he was holding up a beer can while kissing a woman I took to be his dear old mom on the cheek. *How sweet.*

Like Peggy Smart's house, there were no books anywhere to be seen, but there was a sixty-four-inch flat screen television and a PlayStation, so someone in the Olley household was making money. I wondered who it could be.

"Is there anyone else at home?" Lonnie asked, snooping further back into the house.

"Hey! If you want to look around, you're gonna need a warrant," Reginald replied angrily.

"I have no interest in what you've got going on in your mother's house, Mr. Olley," I said. "I just want to talk to you about Cassandra."

"So talk," he said, as he flopped down on the couch.

I pulled my iPad from my pocket, entered my code, and opened the Dictaphone app, turned it on, and informed him I'd be recording the interview.

"Do you have any objection?" I asked when I'd finished the canned speech.

"Would it make any difference if I did... Nah, go ahead. I don't give a shit."

I recorded the date, time and who was present and then I asked him what he remembered about the night Cassandra died.

"I think Peggy killed her and I told her so..."

"You're out of your mind," Lonnie said. "She was

stabbed more than forty times. You think her mother could have done that to her?"

Reggie shrugged. "She was jealous of her, angry jealous. You've seen pictures of Cassie. You saw what she looked like." He pulled a pack of cigarettes from his jeans pocket. "She was a lovely kid, but it ain't safe to be walkin' around lookin' like she did... an' actin' the way she did."

"Oh, and how did she act?" Lonnie asked as he continued to wander around the living room and into the kitchen.

"Hey, get your ass back in here. I told ya, you want to search the place, get a frickin' warrant," he said, half rising to his feet.

"Sit down, Mr. Olley," I said, "and answer the question."

"She acted like she was better than everyone else, even her mother. Maybe especially her mother." He lit a cigarette and took a long, deep drag turning almost half of it instantly into ash. "Cassie was a tease. That's for sure."

"And she teased you," I said. "Is that why you told Peggy that Cassandra got exactly what she deserved?" I watched his face fall. It wasn't a drastic change. But it was there.

"The only reason I said that was because Peggy kept saying I had something to do with her death." He cleared his throat. "I don't know if you know this, but nothing is ever Peggy Smart's fault. Everyone owed her something, especially Cassie... See, Cassandra took her body, her youth, her time, her money. Peggy felt like the girl owed her. Maybe she did. I don't know."

"Did you have an affair with Cassandra Smart?" I asked.

"I wish." Reginald scoffed. "Don't think I didn't consider trying. We'd had some fun times playing video games and watching movies. I don't think it would have taken much."

"You'd make a play for your girlfriend's daughter?" I asked. "She was at least twenty years younger than you." Sure, it was a jab, but this guy was gross all around. I couldn't help myself.

"If I didn't think I'd have ended up in jail and at the bottom of the food chain, I just might have. The truth is I just watched her like every other man in Chattanooga did, but I didn't touch her. Not to sleep with her. Not to kill her. Not ever." He finished his cigarette and dropped the smoldering butt into a beer can that had been sitting on the coffee table not far from where I'd placed my iPad.

"Why do you think Peggy would say you might have had something to do with her death?" I asked.

"I told you. She was jealous of Cassie. The kid was young and hot, smokin' hot." He nodded with that glazed-over look creeping into his eyes again.

"Mr. Olley, is there anyone other than Peggy Smart that you think might have wanted to hurt her? Punish her because maybe she turned them down, or embarrassed them?" I asked.

"She had a steady boyfriend," he replied. "They'd gone together all through high school. From what Peggy told me, he wasn't happy she was going away to college. Hell, I wouldn't have been happy to see her go either. But I sure loved to watch her leave, if you know what I mean."

He grinned, exposing his yellow teeth and giving me a wink.

"Mr. Olley," Lonnie said, "you do realize you're a person of interest in a murder investigation? Don't you think you should be taking this interview a little more seriously?"

Reggie turned and looked up at my partner.

"No," he snarled. "Because I didn't have anything to do with it."

It was at that point a door down a hallway opened and a woman who couldn't have been Reginald's mother suddenly appeared. I was instantly alert, leaned forward, my hand on my weapon. I knew what it was like to be taken by surprise in such circumstances—it had happened to me once before—and I wasn't taking any chances.

I swallowed hard and felt the scratchiness in my throat. The air in the place couldn't have been helping.

"You make coffee?" she asked him, as if we weren't even there.

"No," Reggie said without averting his eyes from Lonnie's.

I sensed things getting a little tense between them. "You must be Mr. Olley's fiancée?" I said, rising to my feet, hoping my question would distract the men long enough to cut the pissing contest short.

"I am. You want some?" she asked, bleary eyed.

It was obvious she'd been sleeping. Her brown hair was a mess and hanging over her face. I could see she was trying to conceal a black eye beneath it. There were also some bruises on her arms consistent with someone who had been forcefully grabbed. The signs of domestic abuse never change. Unfortunately, a lot of the women never do either. I could come back in a year and this beauty queen will still be with him. She was also obviously used to Reggie having strangers over because of the fact that there were two strangers in the living room at that early hour and it didn't bother her one bit.

"Yeah, I want some," Reggie said, then looked at me and said, "She ain't got nothing to do with this, either. I met her long after I left Peggy."

"What's your name?" I asked, ignoring Olley.

The woman looked at her fiancé before answering. "You're a cop, right? My name's Dee Hilburt. And I ain't saying nothin' more."

I sat down again.

"I wasn't asking anything more," I replied and turned again to Reggie. "Mr. Olley, on the night Cassandra was attacked, did Peggy act any different? Was there anything going on between the two of them that might have made you think there was trouble between them?"

"Hell, Peggy was always acting up. It bothered the hell out of her that she had such a good-looking daughter, but that was an everyday thing. Cassie couldn't walk into the room without Peggy tellin' her she looked like a slut or a hooker. So no, I don't remember anything different."

I cleared my throat again. "How about the boyfriend? Mark something..." I tried to remember his last name, but it wouldn't come.

"Was there anything going on between them that you know of?"

"His name's Mark Smirin and just like I said. He

didn't want her to go to college." Reggie grabbed another cigarette.

"Who are you talking about?" Dee asked, looking to me and then to Lonnie.

"None of your damn business. Now go make the frickin' coffee," Reggie growled.

"I don't have to do what you say..." Dee was about to argue, but all it took was a look from Reggie and she turned and stomped off to the kitchen and out of sight. I watched her walk away and when I looked back at him, he was staring at me. I had the distinct impression the conversation was about to come to an end; Reggie obviously didn't like how his fiancée was behaving. I pressed on anyway.

"Mr. Olley, when did you and Peggy Smart part ways?" I asked.

"I dunno... Six months, maybe a year after Cassie died," he replied as if he were talking about the last time he got an oil change. "Now, if you don't have any more questions, Lieutenant." His voice was lower than it had been the entire interview.

"Just one more. Where's your mother?" I asked as I leaned down and picked up my iPad. I left it recording as he answered my question.

"At work," he replied.

"Of course, *she* is," Lonnie said, sarcastically. "Keeping you in smokes and beer, is she?"

"Screw *you*," he replied, with feeling.

"Where were you that night, Mr. Olley?" I asked.

"You know where I was. I told the detective at the time. Check your damn records."

"You tell me," I said. "For the record."

"That's bullshit. You know where I was. I was at the AMVETS with a buddy until midnight when they kicked us out. I went straight home from there."

I already knew that, but I was looking for inconsistencies in his story.

"Who was the buddy?" I asked.

At that he grinned, then said, "Joe Hobbs, but he can't help you. He died years ago."

That, I didn't know. "So essentially, you don't have an alibi for that night?"

"Yeah, I do. The detectives talked to Joe at the time and he backed me up... but you knew that, right?"

I did know, and I also knew that while Hobbs did indeed provide Reggie with an alibi, Linus Peete didn't entirely believe it.

That being so, I figured there were a couple of alternatives: one, if Reggie wasn't at the AMVETS, he could have killed Cassandra; the other, he could have been screwing his other girlfriend. Either way, he couldn't account for his movements that night which also meant that neither could Peggy Smart, not that I really believed that she had anything to do with her daughter's death.

I stood up. It was time to go.

Reggie's eyes narrowed as he stared at Lonnie. Lonnie didn't make the situation any calmer by chuckling and shaking his head, either.

"Mr. Olley, if you can think of anything else that might help us, something you might have forgotten about the night Cassandra was killed, please give me a call."

I set a business card down on the back of the chair I'd

been sitting in. I was pretty positive I wouldn't be hearing anything more from him... Well, not until we got a 911 domestic disturbance call from Dee Hilburt... *Where the hell did she disappear to, I wonder?*

Olley didn't get up. He stayed where he was on the couch, watching Lonnie.

"Goodbye, Reggie," Lonnie said, and we walked out the door. "Have a nice day."

"Screw you! Don't let the door hit ya in the ass."

"What a piece of work," Lonnie said as we climbed into the car. "You know he did that to her face, right?"

"Of course he did which leads me to believe he did the same to Peggy and maybe Cassie too. The leopard doesn't change his spots," I grumbled, clearing my throat again. I could feel the soreness spreading from the back of my throat around the side to my ears. Whenever I swallowed there was a slight discomfort that made me clench my teeth.

"What did you think of his performance?" I asked.

"I think he was comfortable in his own home." Lonnie fastened his seatbelt. "I think he was probably into Cassandra a whole lot more than he's letting on, and that neither her age nor the possibility of prison bothered him. I think he was screwing her, and her mother probably knew it, which gives Peggy Smart motive. Him too, especially if Cassie was about to drop the hammer on him. And now we know that neither of them had proper alibis. My money is on Reggie."

"I agree with most of that, but... well, I dunno," I said as I drove up the on-ramp and onto I-24 at 4th Avenue. I was heading for Hamilton Place and the Starbucks there;

I needed coffee in the worst way. I desperately needed something hot to sooth my throat. Tea would probably have been better, but I was a creature of habit. The large black coffee felt good going down. But that little bit of relief was soon nipped in the bud when we got back to the station: Henry Finkle had struck again.

5

"What's this?" I muttered.

The files I'd gone over with Henry Finkle the night before were back on my desk. There were post-it notes sticking out of every one of them, dozens of them.

I picked up the top file and read the first note on the yellow paper, "signature not legible." The second one read "date missing."

Worse, this was not in Finkle's sophomoric print. It was written in the neat, elegant script of Chief Johnston's secretary, Cathy. The thought that she had to go through each of these files searching for I's to dot and T's to cross made me want to crawl into a hole and pull the dirt in on top of me. She was probably cursing my name the whole while because it isn't like she didn't have enough on her own plate to keep her busy. I knew I'd screwed up again, big time.

I shut my office door and picked up the phone and dialed her extension.

"Chief Johnston's office," she answered.

"Cathy, it's Kate. I'm so sorry you had to go over these files. Had I known—"

"It's all right, Kate. A little time off the computer is a welcomed respite," she replied in a hushed voice.

"Had I known Finkle was going to dump them on you like that I would have gone over everything again myself. He asked for them and, as usual, he wanted them yesterday. Hell, Cathy, I was in a hurry and... well, you know how he is. I'm so sorry."

I didn't want to complain to her too much. The less she knew of how I felt about Finkle or anyone else the better off we'd both be. It wasn't that I didn't trust her. She was an absolute doll. But I'd never want her to feel the need to lie or cover for me. I was the cop. I was supposed to be the protector, not her.

"Really, Kate. No worries."

"I owe you one, Cathy. I won't forget it."

I hung up the phone and stared at the file folders. If this was the kind of micromanaging Finkle was about to embark upon, I was in big trouble. Police work is never the same thing twice. Sure, we all fill out the same forms but each one is its own animal. There is no standard, run-of-the-mill crime. There is no routine investigation. We followed certain steps, but they always lead us in different directions, never the same place twice. There is no cookie-cutter procedure in any police station anywhere in the world.

My sore throat had crept up into my ears and now I was feeling that sting of my eyes watering. I was coming down with one hum-dinger of a cold. It was November after all and there was a chill in the air.

I grabbed the first file and grabbed a pen from the mug on my desk and started making the corrections and adjustments Cathy had marked. It took me until lunchtime to get everything finished. Not because there were that many things to fix but because I'd convinced myself that if I didn't go through all of these files again, I'd have them right back on my desk tomorrow.

Suddenly, I felt sorry for myself, and the need to call Harry.

Don't do it, girl, I thought. *You've been strong for so long. Just don't do it.*

Harry Starke had been such a big part of my life for so long that when I cut him loose a few months earlier, I'd felt like I was cutting off one of my arms.

But he was always there when I needed him, and right at that moment I needed him... The problem was that he was also there when *other* women needed him.

He'd called, often, and I'd answered, and we'd talked and sometimes I'd... well, I fell for it. But I think he finally got the hint that I needed—what is it all those trashy women's magazines call it? A little *me* time.

I wasn't sure how much me time was required but my gut told me I hadn't had enough yet. Of course, my heart told me enough is enough already and that a woman can't live on bread alone.

But I had come a long way... And besides, now that my throat was sore and my eyes were watering it was just a matter of time before I got all snotty and congested. Who the hell wants to reunite with an ex-boyfriend when the Ebola virus could be lurking just beneath the surface? Not me.

I took a sip of my coffee and stacked the completed files on the credenza under the window out of the way, and there they were going to stay until Finkle asked for them. I wasn't going to go out of my way to return them to him. They could stay there until hell... well, you get the idea. I was totally pissed.

With a deep sigh I opened my iPad and began to make notes on my conversations with Peggy Smart and Reginald Olley. I compared them with their statements after the crime had been committed.

Peggy hadn't implicated Reggie at the time. She was quoted as saying she was sure Cassie's boyfriend had something to do with it. *Hmm, so now we have three suspects. Mark Smirin and the gruesome twosome.*

"Reggie didn't become a suspect until after they broke up. Typical," I mused out loud. "Could it be true that Peggy was more involved than they initially thought?" *Forty-four times?* I thought, shaking my head at the enormity of it. *Her mother? I can't see it, but then again... I've run into some really crazy women. It's possible, I suppose... She didn't seem to have that much anger in her... but who the hell knows? Neither did Ted Bundy.*

Every cop knows it's the worst experience, having to tell the family about the death of a loved one. Especially when it is as violent and cruel as this one was. A good cop can learn a lot from the reactions of the receiver of such bad news. *Hmm... I wonder...*

Lieutenant Linus Peete was the cop who'd knocked on Peggy Smart's door that day back in 1992. I wondered what his gut had told him, if anything. He was probably retired now, but what the hell, I figured it was worth a phone call.

After some digging I managed to scare up the note I'd made of Lieutenant Linus Peete's phone number.

"Hello?" His voice was clear and had a boyish sound to it even though he had to be in his late sixties.

I introduced myself and told him that I was working the Cassandra Smart case and had a few questions.

"Damn," he said, resignedly. "I'd hoped I'd never hear that girl's name again. It was horrible what happened to her, a real shame. But I never was able to get a handle on it. There was something wrong with that girl, and her mother... and... all of 'em, the entire bunch."

This was turning out to be more interesting than I thought.

"I spoke with Peggy Smart yesterday," I said, "and I had the strongest feeling she was hiding something, that there was something about her reaction and behavior regarding Cassandra's death that just wasn't right. Did you ever get any feeling that she might be involved in her daughter's death?"

"Lieutenant," he said, "how the hell would you feel? Her kid was horribly murdered. Look, I don't think it is right to judge anyone's reaction to the death of their child." He cleared his throat. "It has to be the worst experience, bar none, on the face of God's green earth. So I can't, won't answer that."

Sheesh, what the hell kind of investigator was he?

I thought for a minute, then said, "Reginald Olley said he thought Peggy Smart had something to do with her daughter's death. But Peggy also said the same thing about him."

"Once again, Lieutenant, you are judging a grieving drug-addicted mother and hearing the words of a convicted felon."

I closed my eyes, shook my head, then said, "And you won't even give me a hint?"

"All I'll say is that there just ain't enough normal to go around for that entire group."

"What do you mean?"

He let out a long sigh before he continued. "Cassandra was smart, if you'll pardon the unintended pun. She was looking for a way out of that life and, up until that night, it looked like she was going to make it. But she took after her mother; she had a big mouth and had a real problem keeping her opinions to herself. She didn't have many friends; alienated everybody she came in contact with. She'd made a list of complaints a mile long about other students at the university. A habit she perfected in high school. Heck, if a girl just looked at her cross-eyed, she'd have their name in the Dean's ear pronto. It doesn't please me to speak ill of the dead, but from what I learned Cassandra Smart was a beautiful, intelligent, promiscuous, pain in the ass who finally crossed the wrong person."

"You sound like you agree with Reginald Olley that she had this coming to her." I was having a hard time understanding Peete's hostility.

"All I'm saying is that if you leave your front door open, you are asking to get robbed. That doesn't mean you deserve it. It just means you've set up the game, so don't be surprised when someone comes to play."

He cleared his throat again. Maybe he was coming down with a cold, too, and wasn't in the right frame of mind to talk. I'd never known anyone, let alone a homicide detective, discuss a case with so much disinterest. It kind of made me think Lieutenant Peete was... Hell, I don't know what I thought.

"I'm sorry, Lieutenant, if I sound pissed," he said as if reading my mind. "But I am, and I was. Back then I was so pissed I couldn't see straight. I just hate to see waste. And that's what the Cassandra Smart case was, from beginning to end: Wasted lives. Wasted time. Wasted resources. But it didn't end, did it? As I said, I never could get a handle on it. I hope you have better luck than I did. Goodbye, Lieutenant."

And that was that. The other end of the line clicked in my ear; the conversation, such as it was, was over. And I was none the wiser.

What the hell? Who acts like that?

I pinched the bridge of my nose and my eyes burned as they watered again.

So, Lieutenant Peete wasn't going to offer any assistance. I thought about looking into his background but my gut didn't give me the feeling he was hiding anything, and I was a firm believer in the policeman's intuition. I got nothing from Linus Peete. Literally and figuratively.

You could call Harry and ask him if Tim could do a little research for you.

I couldn't believe my conscience was turning on me again. Of course I could call Harry and ask if his resident geek, Tim Clarke, could do a little digging on Linus Peete and heck, anyone and everyone else involved in the Cassandra Smart case. But I hadn't long broken up with him then, and it would mean I had to ask him for help. Oh, I knew he wouldn't say no, but then I'd owe him and the last thing I wanted right then was to owe Harry Starke anything.

My cold was starting to affect my judgment... and my emotions. I needed some medicine, preferably the kind that would knock me out cold. *Geez, Kate,* I thought. *Knock it off. Stop feeling sorry for yourself.*

I got up from behind my desk and went to find Lonnie. He was in his cubicle, lately redecorated with images of guys lifting dumbbells and motivational sayings like *Just Do It* and *No Pain, No Gain.* A year ago, he'd had nothing on his walls, but there would have been at least one empty box of donuts on his desk.

"Hey. I need you to run background checks on Peggy Smart, Reginald Olley and Mark Smirin."

"Mark Smirin? Yeah, I was wondering about him," Lonnie said, scribbling down the names.

I nodded. "Cassandra's old high school sweetheart. We need to talk to him, and I'd like to know all about him before we do... And one more thing: see what you can find out about Lieutenant Linus Peete, late of this department. I just talked to him. It wasn't the most enjoyable conversation I ever had, and I was wondering what happened to him back then... Look, I've got an errand I need to run, and then I'm going to call it a day. If I don't take something for this cold, I'm going to be absolutely worthless."

"I'll have something for you first thing in the morning," Lonnie said.

I knew he would.

Now, I just had to sneak out of the station without being seen by Finkle. I was sure he was going to be looking for me and those frickin' files. I decided it was better for me to leave through the garage exit. I'd come out of there smelling like car exhaust fumes or worse but at least the chances of him loitering around with the mechanics was pretty slim.

And that's what I did, and I thought I was hot stuff having given him the slip like that. But the next day he made sure I knew that he knew what I'd done and that I wasn't going to get away with it.

6

When I pulled my car into the parking lot the following morning, I felt my heart sink to my stomach. Finkle was just getting out of his car and had spotted me.

He drove a red Mustang—wouldn't you know it—and was parked in the front row of the lot reserved for the Chief, Assistant Chiefs, their secretaries and visitors from the Mayor's office or whatever. He saw me as soon as I pulled in and stood, waiting.

"Oh, come on," I muttered. "Give me a frickin' break."

I'd parked just two rows back. My cold hadn't gotten any better, not even after drowning myself in some fizzy cold medicine and taking a hot shower. I'd dressed for success that morning: I put my hair up in a tight bun, white blouse, black pants, black pumps with three-inch heels, and a Lamarque, cream leather moto jacket that had cost me almost a week's pay. I figured I might as well try to look good even if I felt like hell. Even so, I could have used another couple of hours of sleep and I was sure my eyes, red and itchy, showed it.

As soon as I got out of my car, I felt Finkle looking me over. It was like have a snail inch its way down my back.

"Late night, Lieutenant?" He smirked.

"Not quite." I sniffled as I walked past his car toward the entrance.

"Oh, that sounds like a bad cold." He shook his head as he started to walk with me. He had to know how creepy he was, right? He had to know that most people, women, were grossed out by him. "You want me to swing by your place tonight with some chicken soup? Maybe a hot toddy."

"No thanks," I muttered.

"I've never had anyone complain about my bedside manner," he insisted, licking his lips and chuckling.

I was becoming angrier by the minute. *Why the hell didn't I call in sick? But cops don't call in sick. Cold? What cold?*

"Not to your face, anyway," I replied and was about to hurry into the building ahead of him when Chief Johnston appeared in the doorway, and he didn't look happy. What could it be now?

"Lieutenant Gazzara, I need you in my office right now," he snapped.

"Morning, Chief," I snapped back at him. That was the cold talking.

"Henry, my office." I watched as the little weasel nodded dutifully, without a word of complaint and strutted like a peacock ahead of me to the Chief's office.

It didn't bode well for me: no day ever started out well in Chief Johnston's office.

Once inside his office, I took my usual seat in front of the desk. Henry slithered in behind me and to my right where he sat down on a small leather couch. Chief Johnston didn't actually slam the door. Without saying a word, he took his seat behind his desk.

I sniffled loudly.

"You should get something for that cold, Lieutenant," he said, as he picked up a sheet of paper from an open file on his desk.

"I don't need to tell you about the complaint that has been filed against you for—" he began.

"For unnecessary use of force and foul language," I muttered, interrupting him, shaking my head. "No sir, you don't. But as I said in my report, I deny all charges. The guy has a rap sheet a mile long. He didn't give his real name and address and he was confrontational when I was making the bust. He's a proven liar and—"

"Internal affairs doesn't care about his rap sheet, Lieutenant. Neither does the press."

"Chief, this happens to every cop at one time or another."

"Oh does it?" he snapped. "I don't have an investigation into brutality on my record. Neither does Assistant Chief Finkle."

Ouch. That one hurt. I looked to my right out of the corner of my eye and saw him smirking proudly. This was like Disney World and a banana split for him. He was enjoying this entire exchange because he knew I had no way out. There was nothing I could say that would set the Chief's mind at ease. Even though I knew he had my back; Chief Johnston always stood up for his team. He was known for it, but I got the feeling that he was not sure my situation was going to be proven as justifiable force. And if he wasn't sure, it meant that something had turned up in the investigation that didn't look good for me. I looked at Finkle again and I couldn't help but wonder if he had anything to do with it.

"Well, we'll see," Johnston said, quietly. "Now, I understand you had some files returned to you with corrections that needed to be made."

Oh hell. Who let that cat out of the bag, I wonder?

"Yes, sir. I did. Henry here was kind enough to have my files checked and double-checked. I cleaned them up, sir. They're good to go." I sniffed. *That ought to make him happy.* It ought to have done, but it didn't.

He looked hard at me for a long moment, cast Finkle a glance I was glad wasn't directed at me, then said, "You get one pass on this one, Catherine. But I never again want to hear that my secretary has had to step in to clean up your mess. If I do, we are going to have a problem. Is that understood?"

So how the hell did he hear it? Not from Cathy, that's for sure.

I turned my head and gifted Finkle with a look that would have scared away a pit bull. It bothered him not at all. He simply smirked and then, unbelievably, he winked at me.

I turned to look at the Chief. If he'd seen it, he gave no indication of it.

"I understand, sir," I said. My stomach was in knots.

"Internal Affairs will be looking into your latest files. That being so, I need an updated status report on everything you're working on," he muttered.

"I'm current on everything, Chief. Henry knows that."

"I do?" Finkle shrugged and looked at me as if I suddenly sprouted a third eye. "You didn't return any of the files I put on your desk."

"That's true." I swallowed hard. "They are on my credenza."

"Get them back to me immediately."

I nodded, sniffed, and waited.

"That will be all, Lieutenant," the Chief muttered without looking at me.

I got up without saying a word and left the office. If I hadn't felt so damned rotten, I'd have defended myself. But what with the effects of the medicine, lack of sleep, and Henry Frickin' Finkle smirking at me the entire time. I'd turned into a wimpy mess. Not only that, I'd left my coffee in the car.

"Ugh," I muttered as I headed upstairs. It wasn't until I tried to slam my office door shut that I realized Finkle was right behind me. Good thing I didn't mutter out loud what I was thinking of him.

"Oh, for God's sake, Henry. Haven't you screwed with me enough for one day? What is it now?"

"Look, Kate, I really am sorry about what happened back there... This is one of those rare opportunities where we could help each other," he said as his eyes roamed over every inch of me but my face. "You're in trouble this time, real trouble. I don't know if you realize how much. But I can help you. All you have to do is ask."

"Is that so?" I sniffed as I put my hands on my hips and stared back at him.

"Just think about it, Kate. I just might be your best hope at keeping your job." He smiled. "Then again, maybe you aren't really cut out for this line of work."

I didn't answer him. I couldn't. All I wanted to do was smack his stupid face.

Thirteen years on the force, I thought, angrily, *and nothing harsher than constructive criticism in my file. Now, all of a sudden, I'm not cut out to be a cop?*

He stared at me for a moment, then said, "Fine. I want those files on my desk before lunch. Understood?"

He didn't wait for an answer. He turned and walked out of my office. I wanted to slam the door. I wanted to scream, but I didn't do either. I left the door open and sat down at my desk. The files Finkle wanted were already done, but I was damned if he'd get them until the very last minute, not until I was damned good and ready. Instead, I dove right into the Cassandra Smart file. I figured the graphic crime scene photographs, reports and notes would be more than enough to distract me from Henry Finkle, Internal Affairs, and my cold.

"Hey, you need a fix?" Lonnie asked, bearing a tall coffee.

"Careful what you say, Lonnie, or Internal Affairs will be after you, too. But the answer is yes."

"How's the cold?"

"Cold? What cold? Do I look sick? I'm not frickin'

sick," I joked then sniffled and grabbed a tissue from the box on my desk.

"Yeah, right," he said, smiling. "Well, I've got some information for you: Cassandra Smart's mother and the mother's ex-boyfriend."

"Shut the door. Let's hear it," I said, excited to hear something other than criticism.

He sat down and took his dog-eared notebook from his pocket and began to recite his research.

Geez, I thought, *I really do need to jerk him into the 21st century.*

"Peggy Smart was arrested on a couple of drunk and disorderlies. That was after her daughter's death."

"I can understand that," I said before taking a sip of coffee. It smelled good and tasted better and the hot liquid soothed my throat.

"Other than that, she called 911 on our friend Reginald Olley three times. Each time for domestic violence, but she never went through with charges."

"Of course she didn't," I said. "They never do."

"Reginald Olley, on the other hand, has a long list of priors. Aside from Peggy Smart's complaints for domestic battery and assault. He was convicted for an assault with a deadly weapon. Seems he got into a fight at the AMVETS and stabbed a guy; that one got him twelve months in Silverdale. Seems he has a bit of a temper. There was also another incident where a knife was involved. Apparently, he beat up his live-in girlfriend at the time, a Gina Torez, and threatened to kill her with a kitchen knife." Lonnie shook his head.

"Okay. And?"

"Torez never showed up for court and so the charges were dropped." Lonnie looked at me. "So Reggie likes to use a knife, and people like him don't ever change, right?"

"No, they don't," I said, and took another sip. "One more strike against Reggie. He had motive, and we've got that on record, and he has a history with a deadly weapon. We can't, however, place him at the scene... Okay, for now, we'll move him to the top of the list. What else have you got?"

"Well, I ran Mark Smirin's name and seems that he's got a bit of a temper, too." Lonnie scratched his head. "One count of simple assault against his girlfriend."

"That's a misdemeanor," I muttered.

"Alcohol was involved. He paid the fine and he's been clean ever since."

"Who'd he assault, and when?"

"Cassandra, fourteen days before she died." He looked at me slyly.

"Holy shit! So you're telling me he assaulted her just before she was murdered? What the heck? There's nothing about that in the file. Please tell me you've got a current residence for him?"

I frowned, thinking that with my present streak of bad luck that he'd probably moved to Alaska.

"I could only find his mother's address. She still lives here in Chattanooga."

"Let's take this coffee to go." I didn't tell Lonnie how happy I was for the excuse to get out of that office. I grabbed my iPad and keys and before my coffee even had a chance to cool, we were driving to the home of Mark

Smirin's mother... and yeah, I forgot about the files and Finkle.

Thankfully, Mother Smirin lived in a better part of town, on McBrian Road off Brainerd Road, a busy strip that dissected the city from McCallie Avenue to Highway 153. Brainer Road was a world of payday and title loan companies, restaurants, bars, used car dealerships, pawn shops, and the like, but the streets that branched off it were, for the most part, quiet; the houses were well maintained, had curb appeal, fences and flowerpots, and a few even had American flags and wind chimes hanging from their front porches.

7

The Smirin home was a nicer one on McBrian. The lawn looked as if it had been professionally landscaped. The driveway appeared to have been recently repaved and the porch recently painted. The curtains were slightly parted in the bay window at the front of the house, and I could see movement inside as we pulled up.

Within a few seconds of getting out of the car I saw the curtains move; we were being observed from inside. Before we could ring the doorbell, however, the front door opened; the screen door remained locked.

"Can I help you?" The woman who answered reminded me a little of Peggy Smart... Well, what she might have looked like if alcohol and a hard life hadn't gotten to her first.

"Mrs. Smirin?" I watched her eyes.

"Yes?" she replied cautiously. Her eyes flitted from me to Lonnie and back again. I held up my badge and introduced myself.

"I'm Lieutenant Gazzara, Chattanooga PD. This is Sergeant Guest. Is your son Mark at home? I'd like to have a word with him."

"May I ask what this is about?" she asked, both hands clamped on the edge of the door.

"Cassandra Smart," I said, watching her eyes. "We've reopened the case. I'm the investigating officer and, according to the file, your son and Cassandra were dating at the time of her death. We were hoping we might talk to him about it."

Mrs. Smirin rolled her eyes. "It was more than twenty years ago. Nothing's changed since the last time you people questioned my son. But please, do come in."

She unlocked the screen door and held it open for us. The inside of the Smirin house was neat and tidy, except for some children's toys lying on the floor of the front room.

"My grandchildren don't know how to clean up after themselves yet," she said, stooping to pick up a Nerf gun.

"How many do you have?" Lonnie asked pleasantly.

"Two. Caden is eight and Cash is six." She was a proud grandma. "Can I get you something to drink, either of you? Water? Tea? Coffee? Anything?"

"No ma'am, but thank you." I said.

"Please, sit down," she said as she sat down on the couch in front of the bay window.

I followed her lead and sat down in an armchair in front of her and to her right. Lonnie remained standing, looking out of the bay window.

"Is your son, Mark, not at home?" I asked.

"No. He doesn't live here anymore. He moved to Polk

County quite a few years ago. I would have thought that after the way you people hounded him after Cassie died, you'd have kept tabs on him," she said in that tone of voice mothers use when defending their children.

"Do you have his current address?" I asked.

"I do. But I can save you some time. My son didn't have anything to do with Cassie's death. He was devastated when he got the news."

Her voice was quiet, but I could tell she was frustrated that she had to defend her son all over again. She quickly scribbled the address on the back of an envelope, tore it off, and handed the scrap of paper to me. I slipped it in my pocket with a nod of thanks.

"What can you tell me about his relationship with Cassandra?" I asked, looked at Lonnie, and nodded.

He nodded back, sat down on the window seat, and opened his note book.

Mrs. Smirin took a deep breath and clasped her hands, interlacing her fingers.

"They'd been dating since they were sophomores in high school," she began. "Mark was a lot like his father. He had a job as a mechanic since he was sixteen and wanted to stay close to home. He loved cars. Still does. I guess he envisioned a life with Cassandra beginning and ending right here. She, however, had other ideas."

"Mark was charged with assaulting Cassandra two weeks before she was found dead," I said.

Mrs. Smirin winced and shook her head.

"He was. She'd told him that she was planning to transfer to another college, out of state. I think she wanted to escape the reputation she'd built for herself here. He was devastated... and you know how men can be, Lieutenant. You're a pretty woman. I'm sure you've had more than one admirer who was more interested in you than you were in him."

Inwardly, I shuddered as I thought about Henry Finkle.

She looked down at her hands then back up at me. "I told him to let her go, to leave her alone. If they were meant to be together, they'd find each other again." She took a deep breath, closed her eyes and shook her head, then opened them and looked at me.

"Truthfully, I was hoping he'd give up on her. She wasn't exactly what I'd hoped for my boy. But he couldn't bear it. He thought he'd be able to convince her to change her mind."

"So he went to see her, to ask her to change her mind?" I asked.

She half-nodded, then said, "Not exactly. He went first to his buddy's house, someone to talk to, I suppose, and have a few beers, so he said. Unfortunately, he had one too many and made up his mind to try and persuade her to stay with him. It was a bad move," she mused. "But what Mark did was an honest mistake, a bad choice, and he paid for it. That's all; he didn't do anything like those other boys did and they never spent a minute in a jail cell or paid a nickel in fines. But it's not what you know, is it? It's who you know, right Lieutenant?" she asked, bitterly.

I looked up at Lonnie who shrugged. "What boys are you talking about, Mrs. Smirin? No wait. I'd like to record this, if it's okay with you," I said as I took out my iPad.

She nodded. I turned on the app and again asked her permission to record the conversation.

"You were about to tell me about some other boys. Who were they and what did they do?"

"You're kidding me, right?" She choked slightly. "Eddie Winston, Haden Rich and Tim Overbeek. Especially Tim Overbeek."

"Overbeek? Is he any relation—" I started but Mrs. Smirin quickly cut me off.

"Any relation to Mayor James Overbeek?" she asked, through her teeth. "Tim is his son. He has a good job with the city management now, *and* he's also on the Liquor Control Board rubbing elbows with the senators and representatives and—well, maybe greasing their palms would be more of an accurate description. See what I mean? It's *who* you know."

"Was Mark friends with Tim Overbeek and the other boys you mentioned?" I asked. I was puzzled since there was no mention in the file of anyone other than Mark Smirin and a fellow by the name of Kyle Hendrick I had yet to even look into.

"They knew each other, yes. I don't know if I'd say they were friends." She cleared her throat and shifted in her seat before continuing. "Mark knew Tim and the other boys in high school. They were all in the same grade. I guess Tim didn't want to stray too far from his daddy's influence or protection, so he went to UTC.

"Mark said he knew Tim was interested in Cassie..."

She frowned. "And, let me tell you, there were a lot of boys interested in Cassandra Smart from what I'd heard over the years. I'm surprised she didn't respond more positively to Tim knowing where she came from. That would have been a huge step up for her."

I pinched my eyebrows together but before I could ask Mrs. Smirin what she meant, she jumped right in.

"I know what you're thinking, Lieutenant. That I thought Cassie wasn't good enough for my boy." She shrugged, and then continued, "Truthfully, I didn't think she was a bad girl, and I didn't believe half the rumors I heard about her having boys on the side or being wild." She took another deep breath. "I just thought she'd be more trouble for Mark than she was worth. No one wants to see their kid hurt. The kindest thing Cassie could have done for Mark was break up with him... and she did."

"But he didn't see it that way," I said.

"No. He blamed himself for what happened to her. He felt he should have been a man and protected her. Walked her home or called her a cab. The police were eager to blame him, too." She looked at me with hard eyes. "He was heartbroken. He was angry. But he didn't hurt her. That night when she died he was as sober as a funeral procession and in the morning when the police arrived, he told them everything he knew. He told them about Tim Overbeek and that he'd been chasing after Cassie for years. But was *his* name in the papers? No, of course not." She shook her head, angrily.

"You said Mark had never done anything like Tim Overbeek and what those other boys had done. What had they done?" I asked, not even realizing I was leaning forward to hear her.

"Oh, well, let's see. When Mark was in his third year of high school, Haden, Eddie, and Tim—Tim was the ringleader—they made their own little publication rating the girls at the school. I'm sure I don't need to explain what they were rating."

I raised my eyebrows.

"Those boys were on the wrestling team. Mark was not. There were rumors of hazing the junior players that went above and beyond anything done on a college campus that I'd ever heard of," she continued.

She tugged at the sleeve of her blouse. "Then there were the parties. Funny. When I was a teenager parties consisted of dancing and laughing and food. The parties at Tim Overbeek's house were invitation only. Mark only went to one, at least that's what he admitted to me. He brought Cassie as his date. It was their senior year. Neither one of them had ever been to the Overbeek house before. Or since."

"What happened at the party?" I asked.

"Apparently, what happens at every Overbeek party. They get drunk. They lose their inhibitions and... well, they make stupid mistakes."

"Did something happen to Mark at this party?" Lonnie was writing notes as he listened.

"Not that he ever told me. But something happened to Cassandra."

"What?" I asked.

"I don't know. Mark said she wouldn't tell him. They'd gotten separated. The Overbeek house is huge, as you might expect. Whatever it was, Tim and his friends had something to do with it. I think they must have raped her... Well, whatever happened she took it to her grave. Oh, how horrible. That poor, poor girl." She wiped her eyes with the back of her hand; they were watering.

"And no one reported it?" I asked, stunned at the revelation. "No one investigated anything about the underage drinking?" I knew the answer to this question, but I wanted to hear Mrs. Smirin's take on it.

"What? Call the police on the Mayor's son? You're joking, right? Look, I was at La Mond, a beauty shop on Warehouse Row some years ago. She was there... Mrs. Overbeek. What a loud mouth... Anyway, I heard her say she couldn't stop her son throwing parties while she and her husband are away. That it was the responsibility of the other parents to not let their kids go if they were so worried. That's a politician's wife if I ever heard one."

"Cassandra Smart filed a complaint against your son. Why do you think she didn't file a complaint against Tim Overbeek and his friends if something bad happened at this party?"

Mrs. Smirin leaned back in her chair, folded her arms and looked at me, her eyes wide, and said, "Oh, I think she did file complaints against them. But no one ever followed up on them. To the powers that be back then, Cassie Smart was a nobody, and I think that's probably the reason it's now your case, Lieutenant. But I can tell you now, you're not going to solve it. You'll run up against... well, the same road blocks that nice Lieutenant Peak, I think his name was, ran up against are still in place. No, you aren't going to find anything. Mayor Over-beek will make sure of that."

"You don't have much faith in our justice system," I replied.

She nodded. "Damn right, I don't. Look what happened to Kyle Hendrick. Tim Overbeek and his friends locked him in a dumpster and left him there. He almost died, and I'm not exaggerating. He was in that thing for hours before some good Samaritan let him out. That stunt did get into the media, but not the names of course; they were after all *minors*. Anyway, it was covered up and faded away just like the rest of their antics."

I had decided I'd heard enough. This was all I needed. Another cover up. It wasn't bad enough that I had Internal Affairs breathing down my neck for police brutality. But now I was going to have to go peeping in on the backstory of some politician's kid. That just couldn't turn out well. I could feel it in my bones along with the ache of the cold that was getting worse by the minute.

"Well, we do appreciate your help, Mrs. Smirin." I stood up, tapped off my iPad and picked it up off the table.

"Lieutenant, my boy might not be a saint, but he had nothing to do with Cassandra's death. He loved her." She stood up. "Regardless of what anyone said or thought of her. You'll see when you talk to him yourself."

I nodded. "We'll be in touch... and, Mrs. Smirin, if you think of anything else, even if it might seem stupid or insignificant, anything at all, please call me." I handed her a business card.

"I will. Lieutenant, I hope you are strong; you're going to need to be."

I squinted at her, tilting my head to the right in question.

"You're going to be fighting City Hall, and your own department," she said. "Literally. You can bet on it."

"It won't be the first time," I said. But I couldn't let on that I'd been involved in one cover up already. That would be bad for public relations, bad for my career, and bad for my already wobbly health.

I slammed my car door shut, turned the key and fired up the motor and then let loose with a string of obscenities that made even the worldly Sergeant Lonnie Guest blush.

"What the hell have I gotten us into, Lonnie?" I asked as I drove out onto the street. He didn't answer. Hell, what could he say?

I drove on for maybe a couple of miles, gripping the steering wheel tightly, like I was afraid it would escape.

"Shit. I can't do this, Lonnie. You drive." I pulled over into the parking lot of a gas station and switched seats with my partner.

"We've got the names to run," he said as he pulled out of the lot and onto the street. "I'll take care of that as soon as we get back to the office... Look, Kate, just because this Tim Overbeek is connected doesn't mean he's done anything, not since. He sounds like a jerk but maybe he's grown out of it. It was a long time ago. We all did stupid things in high school."

"Really? What did you do?" I sniffled.

"I dated Rosemarie Fanatella, for one," he said, wryly

and shook his head then he turned, looked at me and winked.

I couldn't help but smile.

"You devil, Lonnie," I said. "I didn't think you had it in you."

_____

8

While I was listening to Mrs. Smirin's story I was, so it seemed, temporarily relieved of my cold. As soon as Lonnie and I got back to the office, however, it had returned and I was beginning to feel like I'd just crawled out from under a ton of bricks.

"I'll run those names." Lonnie said.

"Great." I sniffed. The Kleenex I had in my pocket was a shredded mess. I'd have been better off using my sleeve. "I'll be in my office.

As soon as I stepped inside, I saw those damn files still sitting there on my credenza. I glanced at my watch and groaned. It was a little after twelve. I scooped up the folders just as I was gripped with a coughing fit. Since these were going back to Finkle's desk I didn't bother to turn my head. *You're welcome, Henry!*

Fortunately for me, he wasn't there. He must have gone to lunch. The guy was nothing if not punctual. Anyway, I dumped the files on his desk and skedaddled out of his office, hoping to hell I wouldn't run into him on my way out. I didn't.

When I returned to my own office a couple of minutes later, my cell phone was ringing. I glanced at the screen. Harry Starke.

"What do you want Harry?" I muttered to myself as I debated answering the call. The man was a thorn of temptation in my side. I was feeling lousy and at that particular moment, a little tender loving care would have been more than welcome. Hell, it wasn't like I had people banging down my door with pots of chicken soup and get well soon cards.

Yeah, but his kind of TLC you don't need.

My conscience was ruining everything. In two more rings it would go to voicemail. And still I hesitated. I had all kinds of medicine in my system and I knew I looked a mess. Lonnie was too nice to mention it but I sure as hell could see it in Finkle's eyes. I was sure the SOB had been trying to count the number of germs crawling about on me.

Ah, what the hell.

I hit the green button and wouldn't you know it? The call went to voicemail. *All for the best I suppose.*

I flopped down in my chair and waited for the phone to ping and let me know I had a new voicemail message... And I waited, but the ping didn't come. Harry didn't leave a message.

"Fine," I muttered, angry with myself that I'd even considered dropping everything to answer the phone. *Screw him!*

I took a deep breath, stared at my iPad and decided to

get a grip on myself and review my interview with Mrs. Smirin.

I turned on the machine and once again became enthralled with the woman's story. I know that it's every mother's job to defend their kid. But the facts didn't look good for her son, Mark Smirin. The long relationship with Cassandra, the break-up over her decision to leave him, was one strike against him. Not exactly a ball-breaker, but the assault charge... that one was hard to brush off. It proved he had a temper... And that he had a motive.

"If I can't have you, no one else will," I muttered to myself. "How many times have I heard that one? Too many to count. It's one hell of a strong motive: passion, jealousy, vengeance, hate, love—you name it." My voice sounding fuzzy and far off in my ears. *So now we have three suspects,* I thought as I continued to write up my notes.

I was so lost in the moment I barely heard the gentle rap on the door.

"You ready to hear what I found?" Lonnie asked as he stuck his head inside. I could see he had several files in his hands.

"That didn't take long," I said as I glanced up at the clock. "Geez. That can't be right? It's almost three? Time flies when you're having fun."

"Yes. I was having fun," Lonnie said as he came in, closed the door and took a seat in front of my desk.

"I can hardly wait," I said dryly. "What did you find?"

Lonnie cleared his throat as if he were about to thank

the Academy and all the little people who made this moment possible.

"Eddie Winston. He had a rock-solid alibi for the night Cassandra went missing. He was at a kegger. Surprisingly, he wasn't very drunk and had several witnesses to attest to his whereabouts. He drove his girl-friend home and with the parents blessing stayed the night." Lonnie frowned.

"What unconventional parents," I said, rolling my eyes. "We're sure they weren't covering for baby girl's sake."

"Very sure. Eddie stated that he stayed with his girl-friend because he was afraid to be alone in his own house. His parents were out of town," Lonnie answered.

"He didn't have a party at his house? That one has an inkling of responsibility. Where is he now? Let's bring him in and talk to him."

"He moved to Seattle after he graduated and has been there ever since. No criminal record of any kind.

"Haden Rich died in a car accident in 1993, driving drunk just before his college graduation. He too was at the kegger and cleared by Lieutenant Peete."

"That's too bad. For his parents." I sniffed.

"Mark Smirin owns a construction site in Polk County. He also has no criminal record of any kind, but he has no alibi for that night."

He flipped to the next page and continued reading his notes.

"Finally, we come to Tim Overbeek, son of James Walker Overbeek, one-time mayor of this fair city. He has a few minor misdemeanors for vandalism. Seemed he liked to break things, put his name on things," Lonnie said.

"Sure. Smart criminals always put their names on things." I enjoyed watching Lonnie chuckle.

"But he also had a mean streak. It was Overbeek that tossed Kyle Hendrick in a dumpster and locked him in. He was in there for more than four hours and, according to Officer Michael Quince's statement, he, Kyle, came out of that thing in a state of semi-consciousness, and he was filthy... And he'd... how shall I put it? He'd soiled himself, and it got out among his friends. He was completely humiliated, and it was all down to Tim Overbeek. It was after this incident that the gang of four guys seemed to dissolve."

"What did Kyle Hendrick do?"

"He filed charges for assault against Overbeek but dropped them a few days later." Lonnie looked at me and shrugged. "Didn't give any reason why, but I can guess."

"You think it had something to do with Mayor Overbeek?" I asked.

"I'd bet my pension on it," Lonnie said. "I'd say he bought Hendrick off and then had everyone sign a non-disclosure document."

It was always easy to grab for the corruption angle. Unfortunately, though, it did happen. Another unfortunate truth was that I was in such a foul mood that I was ready to point the finger at just about anyone and accuse *them* of corruption. Or fraud. Or prostitution. Or just plain stupidity. Anything.

"And that isn't all," Lonnie continued. "Mrs. Smirin

was right. Tim Overbeek has a nice job as the Assistant City Manager."

"Assistant City Manager? I've never even heard of that one."

"These guys aren't elected. They're hired based on their qualifications, like *most* city employees." Lonnie's sarcasm wasn't lost on me.

"Right," I nodded. "And, as mother Smirin said so eloquently, it isn't what you know but who you know."

"True, and I guess Tim Overbeek knows all the movers and shakers around here, although not all of them like the way he does business: he's currently under investigation for receiving bribes."

"Doesn't sound like he's changed much since high school," I said, rubbing my forehead. "What do you say we pay them a visit? I'm really looking forward to meeting them both, Mark Smirin and Mr. Assistant City Manager Overbeek. We'll do it tomorrow morning. Right now, I need to go home and get some rest or this cold is going to turn into pneumonia."

"Gotcha," Lonnie said as he stood up. "Do you need anything? I can stop and pick up some medicine or food and bring it by."

"Thanks, but no. I've got everything I need," I replied, thinking of the half bottle of red wine sitting on my kitchen counter. "See you tomorrow, bright and early." *Bright? Not likely. Early? Even less likely.*

"I'll call you if anything changes," I said.

9

But the following morning, I was indeed up bright and early and, thank the Lord, feeling a whole lot better. I even went for a short run before a quickie breakfast of toast and coffee. I made it into the office by seven, well before Finkle usually arrived: I wanted out of there before he could get his teeth into me, figuratively speaking, of course.

I stayed only long enough to grab my iPad, laptop and a couple of files, then Lonnie and I drove the fifty or so miles to Reliance in Polk County where Mark Smirin lived.

The Smirin home wasn't quite as nice as Mark's mother's, but it certainly looked pleasant enough.

It was eight-fifteen when we arrived that morning, and we were only just in time, for as we pulled up in front of the house the man himself walked out of the front door, heading toward a huge white pick-up truck parked in the driveway.

"Geez, Lonnie," I muttered. "I'm glad we made an early start."

"Me too," he said.

Since I'd left the office early the day before, I figured I didn't need anyone questioning me, especially he who shall not be named. So before I went to bed, I texted Lonnie and had him meet me at the office at seven. It was a smart move, but for the wrong reason. Oh yeah, I make those every once in a while—smart moves.

I parked the car in front of the house, intentionally blocking the driveway.

Mark Smirin looked up, annoyed, and pointed to the unmarked cruiser.

"What the hell do you think you're doing?" he shouted. "I need to get out of here."

"Mark Smirin?" I held up my badge and watched him instantly become confused. "I'm Lieutenant Catherine Gazzara, Chattanooga PD. This is my partner Sergeant Lonnie Guest. Can we talk to you for a few minutes?"

His shoulders slumped. "This is about Cassandra, isn't it? My mother called yesterday. She said you were looking for me. Okay, I can give you ten minutes. Go."

"We want to know about your relationship with Cassandra Smart," Lonnie replied. "So how about we go inside and you begin at the beginning?"

He heaved a deep sigh, shook his head, then said, "Okay. But I do gotta get to work, so can we—"

"We appreciate your time, Mr. Smirin," I said, interrupting him. "We know you own the company, so I don't think anyone will complain too much if the boss arrives a little late. Now, can we..."

"Sure, if you insist," he said, resignedly, "but please keep your voices down. My wife's still asleep and I'd like for her to stay that way. She doesn't like to hear about Cassie so..."

"Understood," Lonnie said, nodding and we followed Mark inside his garage where a couch, a recliner, a small fridge, and a coffee table occupied one side of the building, while a Kia Soul was parked on the other side.

"Why don't you sit down," he said, waving a hand at the couch.

I did—Lonnie remained standing—and I placed my iPad on the coffee table in front of Mark and informed him I'd be recording the interview. He shrugged, shook his head, and made a wry face, his eyes lingering on the device for several long seconds, but didn't object.

"So, why don't you start by telling us about your relationship with Cassandra Smart?" I said.

Again, he shrugged, then said, "We were together since my sophomore year." Mark cleared his throat. "I was in love with her; crazy about her. I thought we were going to be together forever. But I don't think I was any different from any other kid suffering from their first case of puppy love. You think you're the only one who ever felt that way."

He looked down at his hands as he spoke of Cassandra. "She wasn't anything like what people said she was. She didn't drink. She didn't do drugs." He looked up at me. His eyes were watering. "Would you believe that I took her out five times before she'd even let me kiss her?"

"Why do you think she had the reputation she did?" I asked.

"Jealousy, pure and simple... She didn't fit in. She was smart... and a smartass, witty, told it like it was. She didn't care what they said about her, didn't deny it either, because she figured that was what they wanted," Mark replied. "And she swore she'd never give them the satisfaction."

"Who is *them*?" Lonnie was scribbling his notes as he stood, taking inventory of everything in the garage.

"Everyone: the other students, the faculty, the baggers at the grocery store, even her own mother... and her mother's live-in boyfriend, especially him. You've seen her picture, right? She was beautiful. I don't think I've ever seen a girl before or since who was that beautiful," Mark mused.

"Don't let your wife hear you say that," Lonnie warned and eyeballed Mark in amusement.

I had to admit it was a weird comment.

"No. It isn't like that. My wife is completely different from Cassie. She's pretty and funny and a great mother." Mark's voice was sharp.

"But?" I watched him.

"No *but*. Cassie and I didn't work out, that's all. Most high school romances don't. She wanted out, to make something of herself, but..." He shifted in his seat.

I nodded and said, "But you did assault her when she told you that. You were arrested for assaulting her," I reminded him.

He shook his head and smiled.

"Am I wrong?" I asked. "Did I get my facts wrong?"

He shook his head. "No, you're not wrong. I was drunk and upset. She'd just told me that nothing around here was good enough for her, that she was tired of the same"—he made quotes with his fingers—"crappy people, and the same crappy places and the same crappy rumors." He looked up at me, and said angrily, "Yeah, I got mad; of course I did. How the hell do you think I felt? I was still just a kid, a frickin' teenager, and I'd just gotten dumped... for the first time? Yeah... I hit her, and I instantly regretted it."

"Yeah," Lonnie said, "handcuffs have a way of doing that. But sometimes the lesson doesn't totally sink in."

"Where were you the night she died, Mark?" I asked.

"Home, watching TV. No, I can't prove it. Mom was visiting her sister in Nashville. I told the police that when they asked me the first time. If you need to know what I said just reread your files. I didn't kill her." His eyes were wide, angry.

"Okay," I said. "So who do you think did?"

Mark took a deep breath, looked at his watch, looked around his garage, as if he might be saying good-bye to it soon if he said what was really on his mind. He was stalling. I knew it and so did Lonnie. It was one of those moments: the first to speak loses. He lost.

"She had made a lot of people mad, made a lot of enemies," Mark muttered. "I don't know why she wanted to go to that party. It was a kegger at some house being rented by a couple guys from the University."

"Why didn't you go?" Lonnie asked.

"I wasn't invited. She was, but not me."

"Was Tim Overbeek there?"

Mark swallowed. "Yes. He was. Look, I've got to get to work."

"Do you think Tim Overbeek had something to do with Cassandra's death?" I said the words loudly and watched Mark look toward the door that led into the house.

"I..."

"Tim Overbeek helped you get a couple of sweet construction gigs, didn't he?" Lonnie asked. "When you were just starting out, in business, and his dad, the mayor, managed to keep all of you out of trouble. You, Haden, Eddie and Tim had some wild adventures as kids, and what about that publication you guys spread around town? And the parties, and the underage drinking? People have gone to jail for less. And what about Kyle Hendrick? You guys locked him in a dumpster. He could have died."

"Look." He was growing angrier by the minute. "I hung out with those guys, sure, but we weren't friends. I spent most of my time with Cassie. And when I wasn't with her, I was working or studying. I wasn't even there when they nearly killed that poor guy. I had nothing to do with it."

"Oh sure, you were just a good old-fashioned Boy Scout. You think we believe that?" Lonnie said, sarcastically.

"Believe what you want. It was Tim who was pissed at Cassie. Not me. I loved her," he said in a whisper. He glanced again at the door into the house.

"What was Tim mad at her for?" I asked.

"The same thing every guy was mad at her for. They

wanted to date her. She not only turned them all down, she humiliated them. As I said, she made a lot of enemies, including Beeky—that's what she called him, pissed him off big time." He paused, looked down at his hands, shook his head, and sighed. "Tim always got what he wanted, except for Cassie. He couldn't get her, and it drove him nuts."

"Your mother said Overbeek and his buddies raped her," Lonnie said. "What do you know about that?"

"Nothing. I knew when I saw her the next day that something was wrong with her, but she wouldn't tell me what it was." He shrugged, looked down at his hands. "I don't know... If I'd have thought for a second that had... I'd have frickin' killed him."

Lonnie looked at me, his eyes wide in question. I nodded.

"So, let me put this to you: suppose they did rape her, and suppose she told him she was going to the police. Do you think Tim could have killed Cassandra?" I asked, leaning forward.

Mark stared at me for a long minute without speaking, then he glanced around at the door, then at his watch, and then past Lonnie and me out of the open garage door. He shook his head and clicked his tongue.

"How the hell would I know? Yeah, I suppose. He could have. He was a wicked little bastard, still is, so I hear... Oh for God's sake, why can't you just let her rest in peace? Everyone gave her hell when she was alive. They never gave a minute's peace, and now you're stirring it up. Ah, what the hell. Screw you. I've had enough. I'm outa here." He stood up. "I've got frickin' work to do."

"We're not done yet, Mr. Smirin," I said getting to my feet.

"Yeah... Yeah you are. If you have anything on me then arrest me. Otherwise, move your damn car or I'll move it for you." He stomped away to his truck, climbed in, slammed the door shut, started the engine and rolled the windows up.

I grabbed my iPad, tapped it and stopped it recording, and then strolled slowly back to the car. I made a big deal of walking around his truck, making mental note of the license plate in case we had to put out an APB, but more to intimidate him than anything else; I had already made photos of the truck with my phone.

I went to the cruiser, slid in behind the wheel, and turned the key, fired up the motor, and eased the car slowly out of his way. I'd barely cleared the driveway when he sped out of his driveway and peeled off in the opposite direction.

"Well, what do you think?" Lonnie asked, as I turned the big car around.

"I think... that the list of suspects continues to grow. I also think we'll learn a whole lot more when we talk to—what did he call him—Beeky?" I sniffled and pulled a tissue from my pocket.

"Aren't you feeling any better?" Lonnie asked.

"Yeah, a lot better, thank you. And I'll feel even better when we catch a break in the case." I paused for a minute, thinking hard.

You know, someone stabbed that poor girl more than forty times. That means there was a lot of rage... and a whole lot of blood. On the killer's clothes, face, hands...

especially his hands, and blood is extremely viscous, makes
everything slippery, and the knife would have been soaked
in it. I wonder... Hmm. I need to check the autopsy report.
Oh well, maybe later.

"You ready to go fight City Hall, Lonnie?"

"Ready as I'll ever be," Lonnie said, as I hit the gas
and sped westward along Highway 64 toward Chattanooga.

Timothy Overbeek's office was located downtown
just a couple of blocks from Harry's office. Any other
time I might have dropped in on him and visited for a
while, but not that day. I was in a mood for a fight, but not
with Harry.

As soon as we walked into Overbeek's offices, I could
see why people might be suspicious of his business ethics;
lush didn't come close to describing it.

"Geez. Even his own father didn't have an office this
nice," Lonnie said, looking around at the dark, wood
paneled walls and the leather seats in the waiting area.

"I should have worn my tiara," I said, dryly.

"You have a tiara?" Lonnie looked at me, smiling.
"That, I'd like to see."

"Don't worry. I'm sure it isn't as nice as yours. Come
on." I walked up to the window that separated the office
from the reception area. I rapped loudly on the thick
piece of sliding glass and held my badge up for the
woman to see.

"Can I help you?" The receptionist was a thin bird of

a woman with spiky red hair and a long face. If I had to guess, I'd say she was somewhere in her fifties. She had a flashy style of dress. The clunky jewelry and red manicured nails caught my attention. It was obvious she made a nice living.

"I'm Lieutenant Gazzara, Chattanooga Police. This is Sergeant Guest. We'd like to talk to Mr. Overbeek."

"Do you have an appointment?" she asked dutifully.

"No ma'am. I don't need one."

"Please have a seat. He's very busy, but I'll let him know you are here." She pointed at the seats behind us.

"I've been sitting all morning." I stretched my neck and rolled my shoulders. "I'll stand. Thank you."

I stood, not because I needed to, but because I assumed that every politician, from dog catcher to Governor of the state, including Overbeek, had a second way out of their office, a bolt hole they could use when someone they don't want to talk to showed up. Maybe I've seen too many movies, but better safe than sorry.

Twenty minutes later Overbeek finally emerged from his office smiling broadly. He'd obviously kept us waiting, hoping we'd leave; we didn't.

He looked like a movie star. The dark blue suit was obviously expensive, as was the shirt and tie. Not that we had much time to take notice, for he came out of his office almost at a run, charged at us with his teeth bared and his hand extended to shake.

"Lieutenant Gazzara. Sergeant Guest. Tim Overbeek. Please, come this way. It's much more comfortable in my office." His teeth sparkled, glinted, under the artificial light, like one of those toothpaste ads you see on TV. He looked like an overfed shark.

"Thank you for your time, Mr. Overbeek," I said as we followed him into his office. He closed the door and offered us coffee, tea or something a little stronger.

"I know you're on duty, but I'll never tell." He chuckled.

His face was deeply tanned, his hair, obviously dyed, a deep golden blond trimmed fashionably long. And, yes, even I had to admit, he was a good-looking guy, but as phony as a... well, you get the idea.

"No. Thank you," I said as I sank into the plush leather seat in front of his desk.

"Very good. Now, what can I do for you?" he asked, as he sat down behind his football-field-sized desk, the teeth, still on show, contrasted sharply with his tan.

Inwardly, I shuddered as I placed my iPad on his desk in front of me. *Damned if he isn't the spitting image of George Hamilton.*

"If you don't mind, Mr. Overbeek, I'd like to record our conversation. I tend to be somewhat forgetful and I wouldn't want to misconstrue anything you might say, so it would be beneficial for both of us, wouldn't you agree?" I smiled sweetly at him as I tapped the screen and turned the app on.

"Well, as I don't even know what you want to talk to me about, yes, I do mind." The smile never left his face, his lips were pulled back to reveal even more teeth. *He looks like a fricking horse.*

"I'm afraid I must insist, Mr. Overbeek. We are investigating the murder of Cassandra Smart. So you can consider this an official interview."

The smile froze, his eyes narrowed, and he slowly leaned back in his chair.

"Now," I continued, "I know you must be busy, so if you would state your name for the record, we'll get this done as quickly as possible."

"My name... is Timothy Overbeek... Cassandra Smart? My God. Are you serious? That's ancient history." He leaned forward, folded his hands in front of him and placed them carefully on the desk, the teeth now hidden behind the tanned lips. He was obviously considering his options.

"Yes, it was a long time ago, I agree, but as you know, her murderer has never been brought to justice. There's no statute of limitations on murder, so what can you tell me about that night she was murdered?" I pushed the iPad a little closer to him and waited.

He stared at it, like it was a snake readying itself to strike, and then he looked at me and shrugged, dramatically.

"It *was* indeed a long time ago, so long in fact that I can't remember. Hell, Lieutenant, I can barely remember what I did last week let alone twenty years ago." He leaned back and rubbed his neck.

"It was twenty-three years ago, to be exact, Mr. Overbeek." I cleared my throat. "You and Cassandra Smart went to high school and college together, didn't you?"

He shook his head, slowly, then nodded and chuckled nervously. "Yes, I guess we did. Yes. Yes. We did."

"Did you ever go out with her?"

"No. She was dating a guy, one of my friends, in fact. And you know what they say, bros before hos." He chuckled again and winked at Lonnie.

"Who was the friend?" I asked.

"Oh, gosh." He snapped his fingers. "Mark. Mark something. I haven't seen him in years. I can't remember his last name."

"Smirin," I said glancing at my notes even though all of this information was in my head. I'd looked over the file so many times it felt like it was imprinted on my brain.

"Yeah. Mark Smirin. Yeah. He used to beat her, as I recall."

"Really?" I asked, feigning surprise. "You remember that, but you didn't remember his name?" I started to write in my small pocket notebook, as did Lonnie.

"Well, that's the sort of thing you don't forget, right? So yes, I remember it. She was trying to break up with him. Every time she tried, he became unhinged. I mean I can see why he'd be upset. She was... something else."

"What do you mean?"

"Oh, you know, Lieutenant. She had a reputation for..." He paused sucked on his teeth, noisily, then continued, "Look, she was... oh, I'm not going to speak ill of the dead. Let's just say that I know for a fact she made good on every promise, if you catch my meaning."

"I'm afraid I don't, Mr. Overbeek. Please explain?"

He rolled his eyes and looked at Lonnie, motioning toward me. "She was easy. Like really easy. I don't think she was faithful to Mark, but he couldn't see it; he was in love with her. Who was I to get in between them?"

"Did she ever come on to you?" I asked.

"She came on to everybody."

"I'm asking if she came on to you. Did she?"

He leaned forward and folded his hands on top of his desk again and looked at me. He was smiling now, a tight thin smile, no teeth.

"No. She never came on to me."

"Did that bother you?" I asked, watching his eyes.

"What?"

"You heard me. Did it bother you that she paid no attention to you?

"No!"

"But you came onto her, didn't you? And she rejected you."

"No, Lieutenant. I didn't, so she never had the chance to reject me. Besides, I never went short," he said, smirking at me. I changed the subject.

"Where were you that night, Mr. Overbeek?"

"What night?"

I sighed and shook my head. "You know very well what night; the night Cassandra Smart was murdered."

He stared at me, then smiled, full of malice. "I was at a party with Eddie Winston and... Haden Rich. I was with Haden until almost two in the morning."

"And Haden Rich is conveniently dead," Lonnie said.

Overbeek didn't answer. He just continued to smile. I didn't bother to follow up, it wasn't worth it. It was as Lonnie said, Rich was dead.

"Mr. Overbeek," I said, glancing at my notes. "You

had some brushes with the law when you were a young man, is that correct?"

"I was a kid. Who didn't? It was what we did, part of the fun."

He leaned back in his chair and I could see the muscles of his jaw working up and down. I didn't let up.

"Tell me about the list," I said. And there it was, the tell, the twitch of his left eyelid. *Here we go.*

"List? What list?"

"You know what list," I said, gently, but staring him right in the eye. "The list, the publication you and your friends put together in high school. Would you like to tell me about it?"

He stared at me through slitted eyes but said nothing.

"Well, I can't say that I blame you," I said, pretending to consult my notes. "Okay, so how about this? You also supplied alcohol to underage kids. Care to share on that one?"

Nothing. He picked up a pen and began scribbling some notes on a small pad that had his name and title across the top. Then he set the pad down, folded his hands and looked at me condescendingly, defiantly.

"No comment, Mr. Overbeek?" I asked. *He's rattled,* I thought. *Hit him again.*

"Okay, so let me ask you this: what happened the night Cassandra attended a party at your parent's house?"

"What do you mean, what happened? We partied, had a few beers, smoked a little dope... It was a party for God's sake."

"I'm told you and your buddies raped her. You want to comment on that?"

"Yeah, I want to comment: it's bullshit, is what it is, total bullshit. We, none of us, touched her."

I nodded. I'd expected nothing less.

"I don't believe you," I said. "I think because she was stupid enough to attend the party without a date you, the three of you, took it as an invitation to the dance, and you gang raped her."

"I don't give a shit what you think," he snarled, his face white with fury. "I've had enough of your shit. I want you out of my office, *now*."

"I haven't finished yet. Why don't you tell me about what you did to Kyle Hendrick."

"Oh, you've gotta be kidding me!" He all but shouted it. "It was a freakin' prank, for God's sake. He was an idiot, a dumb ass. It was just a bit of fun. No harm intended. Everybody does stupid things when they are young. I'm no different from anyone else."

"Different? Oh, you were different. You had the mayor for your dad, and he had the charges erased from your record, and from those of your *friends*." I spit the word out like it was something nasty. "And he paid Kyle Hendrick off, bribed him to drop the charges against you. How much did that cost him?"

I'd seen pictures of wolves snarling into the camera. Their noses wrinkled over their snouts, their eyes glowing, every tooth exposed. I was seeing that same look right then. But he didn't speak. He just sat very still and stared at me.

"Wait, let me backtrack," I said and shifted in my

seat. "How did you know Kyle Hendrick? Was he a friend of yours?"

"No."

"So how? Did he go to the university?"

"No."

Did you know him from high school?"

"Yes."

"Oh. Did he do something to you in high school that made you retaliate? That made you so mad you almost killed him by locking him in that dumpster?"

"I didn't know it had locked." He snarled through clenched teeth. "Look, Kyle Hendrick was just a punk at school. The guy couldn't tell the truth if his life depended on it. He told stories about Guns-n-Roses coming to his house. He said he personally knew Christie Brinkley. The guy was a complete mental-case... Like I said, a freakin' idiot."

"I see. So, Kyle Hendrick annoyed you and was just in the wrong place at the wrong time? Is that what you are saying?" I saw a sheen starting to coat Tim's receding hairline. He was getting more and more nervous by the minute. Lonnie and I were about to get tossed out of his office.

"Did Kyle know what you did to Cassandra that night she died? Did he see you? Maybe he heard you talking to her? Did he threaten to go to the police?"

"I didn't do anything to her." Amazingly, he'd gotten a grip of himself. "I didn't even see her that night. I told you, I was at the party with Haden. Now, we're done. I'm not answering any more of your questions." He pressed the phone on his desk and the scrawny receptionist was immediately at the door.

"Please show these people out, Mary." He looked again at me and said, "The next time you decide to come to my office and make accusations you better have the proof to back it up." He grabbed his pen and began to scribble something on a post-it note, pretending to look busy.

I picked up my iPad, swiping the screen as I walked toward the door.

"One last thing, Mr. Overbeek," Lonnie said. "If you think of anything else you'd like to tell us, we can be reached on our direct lines." He laid a business card down on Tim's desk and with one finger pushed it slowly closer to him. Overbeek grabbed it and quickly tossed it in the garbage can as if it were one of my used Kleenex.

"That's five cents you owe me," Lonnie said. "You want to make it ten? And I've got plenty more." He laid a second card on the desk and repeated the show.

Overbeek ignored him.

"I thought not," Lonnie said. "Have a good day, sir."

"That was interesting," Lonnie said as we walked back to the car. "You pushed him a little hard, don't you think, LT?"

"Hard? I wanted to tear his frickin' throat out... Yeah, it was interesting. I think we need to do a little more digging on our friend, Assistant City Manager Overbeek. I get the feeling there is more to him than meets the eye. The same's true for Mark Smirin... and Reggie Olley, for that matter. Too many viable suspects—four—but no evidence."

"I'm leaning toward crime of passion," Lonnie said. "Cassandra Smart had a terrible reputation. Whether or not she deserved it, we don't know. Her boyfriend says it was just smoke and mirrors but he's the only one that thinks that; everyone else thinks differently which, in itself raises all kinds of red flags. If she was so innocent, there would be others. There aren't, not even her mother. And Smirin was right when he said Overbeek doesn't take rejection well. After our little chat with him, I figure that's a no-brainer. What do you think?"

"My money's on him," I said, "but I think we're going to need a confession. Without that, or the murder weapon... or DNA, we don't have anything on him other than he's an asshole."

"Unfortunately, that isn't a crime," Lonnie said as we pulled into the police department parking lot.

When I stepped out of the car, I had a weirdest premonition that something was wrong. I looked at Lonnie. He winked at me and said he was going to see if he could track down Kyle Hendrick. I nodded and went to my office.

As soon as I stepped through the glass door, Finkle appeared, seemingly out of nowhere, and followed me inside, closing the door behind him. Now what?

10

"**W**hat the hell have you been up to, Kate? The chief is having a conniption. He wants you in his office. Now."

I couldn't imagine what it could be about. I'd been out of the office all morning. I'd given Finkle all the files he'd asked for, even if they were a few minutes late. I'd been playing extra nice with my fellow officers and over the course of several days had even managed to make some of the perps crack a smile. What was this all about?

"What's it about?" I asked. "Do you have any idea?"

"No, but whatever it is, you'd better be prepared. I have a feeling that this time you've stepped over the line."

I looked at him. He didn't look pleased... and for some reason *that* bothered the hell out of me. Any other time he would have been wetting himself with delight at my predicament. *That can't be a good sign. If Henry's feeling sympathetic, I must really be in trouble.*

I sighed, nodded, and headed for the elevator.

"Chief? You wanted to see me?"

"Take a seat, Lieutenant," Johnston snapped.

Finkle had snuck in behind me, closed the door, and then scooted over to his regular cheap seat. He was staring at me, not in that usual undressing me with his eyes look, but with something akin to sympathy. It was unnerving.

"Did you just go and accuse Mayor Overbeek's son of murder?" Johnston asked.

"What? Uh... Wow, that was quick. I just came from Tim Overbeek's office, but I didn't accuse him of anything. His name was in the file as a possible suspect —" Okay, so that was a bit of a stretch, but what the hell? I was in trouble enough already.

"Damn it, Lieutenant," he interrupted me. "Don't you know that Jim Overbeek plays golf every Saturday with Chester Lake, the retired head of Internal Affairs and the father-in-law to the agent who is researching the charges against you?"

I stared in disbelief.

"How on earth could I have known that, Chief?"

The words just slipped out. But it was true. If I kept tabs on every retired person associated with the department, I'd never get any work done. There is always someone who knows someone, right?

"And it wouldn't have made any difference if I had known," I continued. "Overbeek is a suspect in a murder investigation. He gets no special treatment just because of who he is."

"Kate, what are you doing?"

"Chief, I'm trying to solve a twenty-three-year-old murder. Henry assigned it to me, and he's been on my ass

ever since." Okay, so that was a little iffy too, but techni-
cally it was true.

"I never assigned you that case," Henry balked.

"With respect, Henry, you did. We were in the
morgue, remember? You said, among other things," I said,
pointedly, "that I was to get to work on the status of my
files including the one I was holding, the Cassandra
Smart case." Now I was really skating on thin ice, but
since I knew Henry would remember what else he'd said
to me down in the morgue, I was hoping he'd just sit back
and keep his mouth shut. Thankfully, he did. But I knew
he wasn't going to forget it.

"Don't you think it would have been beneficial to run
it past your superiors before heading off to interrogate the
Assistant City Manager?" Johnston asked. "What the
hell was going on inside your head that you thought it
would *not* hit the fan?" The Chief hadn't sat down and
was staring at me waiting for an answer.

"Quite frankly, Chief, I didn't think—"

"You are damn right about that, Lieutenant! You
didn't think. Are you trying to get yourself kicked off the
force?"

Finkle sat still, I figured he must be enjoying the
show.

"No, sir. Of course not," I said. "Tim Overbeek's
name was in the Cassandra Smart file. During the course
of my investigation, I learned from witnesses that he had
quite a reputation and quite possibly had date-raped the
victim. I found it strange that he didn't have a record not
even a juvie. I figured someone was looking after him,
and that it was probably the mayor." I swallowed hard,

thought quickly about what I was going to say next, and then continued, "It would have looked bad, don't you think, if Internal Affairs got the idea that I was deliberately ignoring a potential suspect because of his family connections?"

Of course, what I said was right. But I could tell by Chief Johnston's face that he didn't like being put on the spot like that. There was no way to win this argument. I needed to just take my lumps.

I closed my eyes, shook my head, opened them and looked him right in the eye. "You're right, Chief. I could have handled it better. I should have come to you first, sir."

I looked down and chewed the inside of my cheek.

"But I was just on a roll questioning the suspects. Dealing with city officials is tricky and I didn't want Overbeek to keep ignoring a request for a meeting. So I went to see him. He's one arrogant piece of—"

"That's enough, Lieutenant. You don't even know he would have done that." He scowled, looked at Finkle, then back at me.

"This isn't over, Kate. Not because I want to keep punishing you but because Internal Affairs is going to hang on to it like a bulldog with a bone. You won't skate past it no matter what I do or say."

"I understand, Chief."

"I hope you do," he said, and finally sat down.

"Now, tell me what you are working on, and don't leave out a damn thing. I don't want to be blindsided like this ever again. Do you understand me?"

"Yes, sir. I do."

I brought them up to speed on the Cassandra Smart case as well as a couple other files that I'd wrapped up.

"So, when do you think you'll be contacting Timothy Overbeek again?" Johnston asked, when I'd finished.

"I'm not sure, sir. I have several more interviews to conduct, and I need to go over the crime scene photos and reports again before I decide," I replied, sniffling.

"What's wrong with you, Kate? Allergies?"

"No, Chief. I'm just fighting off a cold. It's that time of year, you know."

"Yes, well, thanks for bringing it into work. We'll probably all have it by the end of the week," he muttered as he scribbled some notes on a legal pad. He too had not yet accepted the new technology. He didn't even have a computer on his desk.

We sat in silence for an awkward couple of minutes. I cleared my throat and waited for Finkle to say something, but he wouldn't wipe his own ass unless he was ordered to by the Chief.

"Lieutenant, go ahead and conduct your interviews. Then I want you to pass the Cassandra Smart file to Henry."

Suddenly I wasn't on the defensive anymore. I was angry.

"What? Why? Uh, sir?"

"If the situation is as sticky as you say it is, it needs to be handled with discretion. If there's anything that has to do with Mayor Overbeek's kid, and if we have probable cause, I want Henry to take the reins." He looked at Finkle who nodded in compliance.

What a frickin' suck-up.

I didn't say anything. What could I say? This was all because of Internal Affairs. All I could do was bite my tongue, literally, and nod my head.

"That'll be all, Lieutenant." Chief Johnston didn't even look up at me.

I was angry, and I should have put up more of a fight, but at that moment I just didn't have it in me.

As soon as I stood and turned to walk out, I could feel Finkle's eyes on my back side. I hurried out, closing the door behind me. Cathy pointedly ignored me as I walked past her desk. She didn't bother to look up from her data entry, even as I swiped two tissues from the box sitting on her desk.

I went to my office, closed the door and the blinds, and flopped down in the seat behind my desk, my ego bruised, my enthusiasm busted.

I thought about what had happened to me over the past several days. Things were going downhill fast. It was a bummer, but on reflection there was nothing I would have done differently. Having decided that, I figured the best thing for me that day was finish the damn case and hand it off to Henry, and the sooner the better.

That was it then. What did I care who got the credit for the case? Hell, I hadn't even solved it yet. All I really knew for sure was that Tim Overbeek acted like a man trying to cover something up. And his father had covered something up. Lots of things, in fact. Tim might be just a jerk and nothing more, but my gut was telling me he was more involved than he wanted to admit.

I tried to comfort myself with those thoughts, but they weren't comforting at all. Once again someone else was going to get credit for my work. Why the hell couldn't the Chief let Lonnie take the lead? Why did it have to go to Finkle? When Lonnie returned, I gave him the Reader's Digest version of what had happened.

"What do you think?" I asked when I'd finished.

"What do I think? Well... fight City Hall, you can't," he said with a fair impression of that pointy-eared, Star Wars alien, Yoda.

Bad as I felt, I had to smile and shake my head.

"It's over, Lonnie. When all is said and done, I'll hand the case over to Finkle: the I's dotted, the T's crossed. He gets the credit. I get the shaft. Internal Affairs will charge me with excessive use of force, and I'll lose my job."

"Don't talk like that," Lonnie said. "Just... just do your best. I know it sounds bad, but the Chief has your back. He thinks well of you, always has. Hell, Kate, you can always go and work for Harry. He's been trying to get you to make the switch for years."

I looked at him in amazement. "Work for Harry? Have you gone mad?"

"Don't give up, Kate. Just don't give up. That's what you told me, remember? And I didn't, and it worked. You helped me, Lieutenant. Finkle can barely look me in the face now that I've lost weight. That's partially because of you. So, now it's up to me to return the favor."

I smiled at him. "Yeah," I said, wrinkling my nose, "but Harry Starke. I don't think so."

I stared at the pile of paper on top of my desk for a couple seconds, then grabbed my notes on the Cassandra

Smart case and said, "Okay. Tell me what you've found out."

Just then my phone rang. It was that all-too familiar number. Harry Starke. *Wow—talk about speaking of the devil.*

"Lonnie, I gotta take this. Put everything together for me and let's tackle this first thing in the morning. I'll swing by your place and pick you up."

"Are you sure?"

"I've been ambushed coming into the station twice in just the past week. I can't take it again. Besides, variety is the spice of life. No cop should ever have a set routine." I nodded. "Especially when Internal Affairs is on your ass."

Lonnie chuckled and closed the door as he left my office.

"Hello Harry," I answered the phone.

"Are you avoiding me?" Harry never was one to beat around the bush.

I took a deep breath. "Avoiding you? Maybe a little, I suppose."

"Why?"

I looked at the phone as if it had suddenly become a writhing snake.

"Did you really need to ask me that?"

"Talk to me, Kate. What's going on? I thought things between us were getting back to normal."

Slowly? Sure. But surely? I didn't think so, but he sounded so sexy on the phone.

"I'm sorry, Harry. I don't really have time to talk right

now. I've got Internal Affairs breathing down my neck and Chief Johnston is on the warpath and—"

"Internal Affairs? What's going on, Kate?"

"It's just the same old story. You know, some thug claiming police brutality. I don't want to talk about it."

"Do you need my help?"

Yes! Tell him yes!

"No, Harry. I don't. But thanks." *You're frickin' crazy.*

"Look, I've got to go. I'll call you when things calm down a little." My little voice inside was screaming obscenities at me.

"Oh, come on, Kate. You can do better than that... Okay. When will you call?"

"I don't know. Later. Just later. Bye, Harry."

I swiped the little red button and sat there for just a moment before picking up Cassandra's file and looking at the high school picture her mother had provided. She was a very pretty girl. It was infuriating to look at the crime scene photo and see what had been done to her. But I'm no different from any other cop. That's what we all feel like when we see the things we see. We get angry. And when we catch a bad guy it sometimes takes superhuman strength to stop ourselves from getting in a lick or two, or even putting a bullet in his ear. That's something no one understands.

Would Cassandra's mother find fault with me for punching Tim Overbeek in the face when I arrested him? I doubted it. How about all of the other victims' loved ones? Would they rush to the defense of the killer and say *Hey, hey, now girlie-girl. Don't get rough with him. He's got feelings too.* Again, I doubted it. But, then again, maybe I'm wrong. Maybe I am the loose cannon everyone thinks I am. Maybe Internal Affairs was right to home in on me and leave the clowns like Finkle alone. I just didn't know anymore. All I did know was that I needed more than a hunch to prove that Tim Overbeek was my man. I needed something solid, something that would put him at the scene. Perhaps Kyle Hendrick would provide me with that something solid.

Idly, I picked up the pile of photos and paged through them, not really seeing them, my mind whirling... and then something in my head clicked. *What the hell?*

I went through the photos again, this time examining each one in turn, and even then I almost missed it. I put the photos aside, all but three, and then I picked up the forensic report and read through it. I found the page I was looking for and again picked up one of the three photos I'd set aside, stared closely at them, then read the two paragraphs again.

They processed the frickin' thing only for prints not blood... The prints all belonged to Cassandra... That bag didn't get on that branch by itself. Someone hung it there... He wanted it to be found... Either that or he was taunting... sending a message, maybe? Why the hell didn't they process it for blood? Doc Sheddon—damn, he's been here forever—said that from the nature of the wounds, the knife had no guard on it. Lots of blood... slippery... excessive force. If his hand slipped down the handle and... oh my God... if he cut himself...

I dropped the photo on the desk and jumped to my feet, adrenaline coursing through my veins.

I almost ran to the morgue where what little evidence had been gathered was stored.

It took a few minutes, but I found it, a cardboard box containing the kid's clothing, underwear, shoes, necklace, a number of small personal items, including a leather wallet, change purse with a number of coins in it, and some items of makeup and other things young girls consider important. It was all pretty unremarkable, except for the expensive dark blue, leather purse complete with a shoulder strap. I grabbed a pair of latex gloves, pulled them on, and carefully lifted the purse out of the box. Even empty, the purse was heavy, and with its contents would have made a nifty weapon.

I examined the purse closely—well, as closely as I could without a magnifying glass—and I found nothing: no blood. I signed it out and took it to Mike Willis, head of the forensics department.

"Hey, Mike," I said, laying the purse gently down on his desk. "I need a favor, please. I need this processed for blood, and I need it done like yesterday."

"And good afternoon to you too, Kate," he said, wryly, while pulling on a pair of latex gloves.

"Yeah, that," I said. "Sorry, Mike, but I think this may be the key to a twenty-three-year-old cold case. And I need a win in the worst way. Can you help... please?"

"I'll do what I can. You know that." He picked up the bag and examined it.

"I don't see anything, but don't panic. Not yet."

He took a huge round magnifying glass from his desk drawer and examined the bag again, then he looked up at me, the glass still up to his face. I burst out laughing. His eyeball was the size of a grapefruit.

"You found something?" I asked when I'd calmed down.

"Yes. Maybe. Give me a couple of days, okay?"

"Yes, okay, that's fine. Thanks, Mike. You're a lovely man and I love you. Oh, and if you do find anything, please run the DNA. It will save time."

"Well, I'll send it to the lab and cash in one of my chips, but I can't promise—"

"I know," I said, interrupting him. "But I have supreme confidence in you, Mike. Later, okay?"

He nodded, and I almost skipped out of his office and back to my own.

I grabbed my iPhone and tapped the speed dial. I felt better in that moment than I had in weeks.

"Hello, Kate," Harry said. "That was quick."

"I know. You want to buy me dinner tonight?"

"Sure. Your place or mine?"

"Neither. How about Ruth's Chris? I could murder a filet."

"You got it. I'll pick you up at eight. That okay?"

"Of course. Thanks, Harry."

11

As you might well imagine, I was late into the office that following morning... Yeah, well, I know, but that night I needed something only Harry could give me, and he did, twice; the steak was good too. Yeah, I know. I used him, and I don't regret it, not for a minute. What would you have done? No, don't tell me. I already know; you'd have done exactly the same as I did, so don't you dare judge me.

Fortunately, Finkle was nowhere to be seen, so I grabbed Lonnie and we headed out to interview Kyle Hendrick.

~

"Do you think Tim Overbeek gave him a heads-up?" Lonnie asked as we stood at the door of Kyle Hendrick's apartment.

I stood on my tip-toes and tried peeking in the peep-hole but couldn't see a thing.

"Maybe, maybe not. We'll see. How far is it to his place of work?"

"Let's see." Lonnie pulled out his well-worn notepad and flipped a few pages. "The First Choice Automotive Mart is on Broad, about ten minutes from here."

"Okay, we'll go through McDonald's drive-thru and get coffee on the way."

We headed back to the car with Lonnie clicking his tongue and smiling as he climbed into the passenger seat. *What's that about?*

"You know something I don't?" I asked as I fired up the engine.

"No... I was just thinking, is all.

"About what?"

"Nothing, honestly... Okay, I was thinking about those eighty-two pounds I lost. It's... It's hard to believe, Kate. I feel like a different person."

"You *are* a different person. Good job, Lonnie. Keep it up."

We pulled onto the First Choice lot. It was a typical "we tote the note" used car dealership: five hundred dollars down and you drive away in a car with an exorbitant weekly payment and a device that disables the ignition system twenty-four hours after the payment becomes overdue. It was a sleazy world of multicolored flags and balloons on the antennas of several dozen used cars. I'd bet a month's salary that there wasn't a vehicle on the lot that had cost the owners more than the down payment.

"You in the market for a new car?" I asked Lonnie.

"From here? Are you kidding me? Hell no."

"It might help us get in there if you were." I was

joking, of course. We had badges that guaranteed entry to almost anywhere we wanted to go. I took a quick sip of coffee before slipping it back into the cup holder and leaving it for later.

"Will you co-sign?" he asked, also joking.

"Uhm, no."

"I really like that Camaro over there." He pointed.

"Ugh. You in a Camaro? You'd have to grow a mullet, and wear jeans, a gold chain, and button-down shirts open to your navel. You think you could carry it off? Because driving a Camaro requires a commitment."

"I could do that," he said, grinning.

"Yeah, right," I said. "You do that and I'll have you transferred to Narcotics so fast it will make your head spin. You'd fit right in."

"Ma-an, you do know how to take the fun out of just about everything, Lieutenant."

"I do, don't I?"

We walked into the showroom and were instantly greeted by a smiley guy with blond hair, a polo shirt, khakis and tennis shoes.

"Good morning. My name is Rob. What can I show you today?"

"Not a thing, Rob," I said, holding up my badge. "We're looking for Kyle Hendrick."

"Kyle? Oh, yes. Sure. He's in his office. Right this way." Rob walked quickly to the back of the showroom to a row of offices that were really nothing more than tiny glass cubicles. Working there must have been like swimming in a fishbowl.

"There," Rob said, pointing to a cubical wherein a man was sitting hunched over his desk.

"Thank you," Lonnie said firmly, making it clear that Rob's services were no longer needed.

Rob took the hint and returned to the showroom.

I knocked on the doorframe. "Kyle Hendrick?" I held up my badge again.

The years hadn't been kind to him. His face was doughy, and he looked as if he could stand to lose a few pounds. His blond hair was thin and receding but the comb-over still managed to cover most of his head. He looked soft all over. He wasn't wearing a wedding ring.

"Yes, ma'am." He stood up, smiling.

"I'm Lieutenant Gazzara. This is Sergeant Guest. We'd like to ask you a couple of questions."

"What about?" He motioned for us to sit down. Lonnie took out his pad of paper from his breast pocket. I produced my iPad and informed him I was going to record the conversation.

"You are? What for? Well, okay... I guess you can. Yeah, sure," Kyle said, as he watched me swipe the locks and enter my code and then state my name, the date, time, and names of those present.

"Mr. Kendrick, what can you tell me about Tim Overbeek?"

"Tim Overbeek? What do you want to know about him for?" Kyle nervously tapped his pencil on the papers he'd been working on.

"Just answer the question, Kyle," Lonnie said.

"I don't know him. I mean, I know of him, but I don't

know him." He tried to hold my gaze, but quickly gave up and looked down at the papers.

"Tell us about the day he locked you in that dumpster," I said clearly for the recording.

Kyle's shoulders shivered as if a cold breeze had suddenly rushed over him. He hesitated, then said, "What's this about, Lieutenant? Overbeek's an ass. I haven't spoken to him in years."

"It's about Cassandra Smart. You remember her, don't you?" I asked as I watched his eyes.

His mouth opened and the color drained from his face.

"Well, don't you?" I pushed him.

"Yeah, I remember her. Of course I do."

"So tell me about Overbeek. Did you have some kind of altercation with him?" I asked.

"You didn't have to have an altercation with Tim to have him lash out at you," Kyle said quietly. "Look, I've got a lot of work to do. I don't have time to talk about things that happened twenty-odd years ago."

"Mr. Hendrick, you don't have to be afraid of Tim Overbeek." Lonnie leaned forward as he spoke. "He can't hurt you. The lieutenant and I will make sure of that. But if you know something that might help us bring justice to Cassandra and her family, it's your duty to tell us."

He sat for a moment, very still, then said, "Tim Overbeek was, is, a bully. Not your average name-calling bully. He was vicious. It was a sport for him. I'd managed to stay out of his way through most of high school..." He stared vacantly at the wall, obviously reliving bad memories.

"I hated high school," he continued. "Everyone had their own cliques and if you didn't fit in, if you were different, there just wasn't any place for you." He took a deep breath, then said, "I think the fact that I'd gone under the radar for so long was what made Tim do what he did."

Kyle shook his head. "Look, he cornered me when I was walking home from the convenience store. I tried to get away from him and run down an alley but I tripped. When I tried to get to my feet, he and his friends were already on top of me. The next thing I knew I was in the dumpster with the lid locked down tight. I told the police all of this when they interviewed me. I'm sure it's in a file somewhere. You can read it for yourselves."

"Mr. Hendrick, do you know if Tim Overbeek had an interest in Cassandra Smart?" I asked, changing the subject slightly.

"Hah! Sure he did. Who didn't?" Kyle replied. "He had a crush on her, but she was seeing someone. Well, from what I heard she was seeing several 'someones.' She might have been a slut... But she was smart, and not just in name. She knew exactly what Tim was and she brushed him off, wouldn't have anything to do with him."

"Were you at the party that night, the night she was murdered?" Lonnie asked.

"No. I didn't go to parties. Not then, not now. I'm not a big drinker."

"Mr. Hendrick," I said. "It was a serious assault against you. You could have died, so why did you drop the charges against Tim Overbeek?"

The room was suddenly blanketed in silence. Kyle

looked at his watch and shook his head. When he looked up at us, he seemed apologetic, the pencil tapping nervously.

"I just didn't want to press charges. Look, the truth is, I didn't want any trouble with the Overbeeks."

"You know something about Tim, don't you?" I asked. "You saw him with Cassandra that night, the night she was murdered, and you're covering for him because if you don't, he'll do worse than put you in a dumpster. Am I right?"

"No, I didn't see anything."

"Mr. Hendrick, if you're hiding something, withholding evidence, you could be charged as an accomplice," Lonnie said.

"I told you. I didn't see anything."

"How can you cover for him after he did what he did to you?" I was tired of playing nice. "You almost died in that dumpster. There was no air, just the stink of all that garbage. You lost control of your bladder, too, didn't you?"

Kyle scowled at me as his cheeks flushed red.

"Tim Overbeek did that to you and still you want to protect him? I don't get it," I said.

"You don't know what it was like. I still dream about it. I just wanted to forget about it!" He dropped the pencil and started to nervously knead his hands. "I wanted to just push it away and never think about it again. And now you two come in here and bring it all back... Sc-rew you, both of you." He had his head in hands, elbows on his desk, eyes closed.

I sat back in the plastic seat and watched Kyle as Lonnie made notes.

"Mr. Hendrick," I said, quietly, "how well did you know Cassandra Smart?"

"I didn't know her hardly at all," he said, his head still hidden in his hands.

"According to the file you told police at the time that you and Cassandra were friends. Why would you say that if it wasn't true? It's not something you're likely to forget, now is it? She was very pretty. She had good grades, too."

He sat up, leaned back in his chair. His face was red. I watched him as he nervously rubbed the meaty part of his left palm.

"Were you friends with her, Kyle?"

"Not really. We talked every once in a while. That's all. She was... nice."

"She was nice to you?" Lonnie asked.

"Yes. Oh, yeah. She was nice to most everybody. She wasn't ever mean. Except to Tim, but he... sometimes, well, he asked for it."

"What do you mean by that?"

"I told you: he was an ass. He'd make lewd comments to her. He did it all through high school. He's always been a bully. But I don't know if he killed her. I don't know if he was anywhere near her when she died. Maybe he was... I don't know."

He wiped his forehead with the back of his hand. He looked like he was about to become unglued.

I looked at Lonnie. His eyes were narrowed, his nose

wrinkled as he studied Kyle. It was as if the man had suddenly started to give off an offensive odor.

Leave it to Lonnie to put the guy at ease, I thought.

"Please." Kyle was nearly begging. "I don't want to talk about it anymore. You've got my statement. I'm at work and I've got things to do."

I swiped the iPad stopping the recording. I stood up, but Lonnie was ahead of me. He dropped both of our business cards on the desk in front of him.

"Mr. Hendrick," I said, "if you think of anything else, anything you might have forgotten, even if you think it is unimportant or stupid, give us a call. You can talk to me or Sergeant Guest."

Kyle picked up the cards and nodded as he stared at them.

We told him goodbye and left the office and made our way through the cars in the showroom and out the glass doors.

"What do you think of that?" I asked Lonnie. We stood outside the car for a few moments. The sky was turning gray; rain was in the air. November weather was upon us.

"I think that Kyle Hendrick needs to confront Assistant City Manager Overbeek and kick his ass."

Lonnie flipped through his notes.

"Did you notice how he kept tapping that pencil? It's like he was suffering PTSD or something," Lonnie said. "He's left-handed too. I read up about that once, a long time ago. As I remember it, there is a higher probability of him being a genius than a right-handed person. Did you know that? Lefties are smarter than righties. So they say."

"Well, I don't know how smart he can be if he let Overbeek just skate the way he did. That seems like a pretty dumb move to me... Maybe, now that he's had the whole thing thrown back in his face again, he'll want to talk. Maybe he'll decide he's got something for us. Which would be good, because right now I'll take anything. And also right now I need my coffee."

I opened the car door, slipped in behind the wheel, and took a long sip of my tepid coffee. I stared at the dealership for a few minutes and let my mind wander.

If the guy didn't want to talk, there wasn't anything I could do. But something else was stuck in my craw and I couldn't figure out what it was. I decided to take another look at the file and see if Sheriff Peete had made any notes about Kyle's behavior that night. It might warrant another phone call to the man although I wasn't looking forward to that. *Hmm, maybe tomorrow... or not.*

12

It was three days later when things really took a turn for the worse. I knew something was wrong as soon as I walked into the bullpen late that afternoon, where the uniformed officers mingled with the detectives and secretaries discussing and tackling their own current cases.

Everyone stopped what they were doing and looked at me. At least that's how it felt. Maybe it was all in my head. But I felt the need to look down and check my outfit for an open zipper or perhaps a button revealing my bra beneath. But no, everything was covered and I continued on to my office.

"Where have you been?" Finkle spoke from the side of the room by the credenza making me jump.

"Yikes, Henry!" I put my hand to my chest.

"Oh, did I startle you? I'm sorry."

Like hell you are.

"No, you didn't." I rolled my eyes and slid behind my desk, keeping the big, bulky piece of furniture between us. "What's going on out there?" I asked. "Anything I should know about?"

"Internal Affairs is making the rounds." He said it like it was nothing more than a visit from his secretary to sign a birthday card for the Chief.

"Oh really. Is there anything I should know?" What was I doing hoping Finkle would throw me a bone of compassion?

He looked at me with a smirk. "What's it worth to you?"

"Come on, Henry. Don't start."

"They are doing their job. Just asking questions and collecting information. That's all."

"You seem really calm about it," I said. "That probably means I'm in deep shit." I grabbed the first file on my desk. "Have you talked to them, too?"

"Not yet. I'm scheduled to meet with them later."

"Later today?"

He shrugged. Of course he did. He was enjoying watching me squirm and sweat. I hated him for it. I hated him for more than that, but he was really getting under my skin.

"Okay, well, if you don't have anything to tell me, Henry, I'd like to get as much work done as I can before I'm bounced out of here."

"Word has gotten to them that you've been harassing Timothy Overbeek."

"Harassing? IA is calling my questioning of a murder suspect harassing? And you let them get away with that?" I fell back in my chair. "I thought this was already being taken care of. I only contacted him a couple of days ago...

well, three. In fact, I was getting ready to pass along my notes and—"

"Calm down. This isn't any reason for you to get all emotional."

"I'm not emotional. I'm still trying to get over a cold. Come on, Henry. How many times have you seen me get emotional? I resent that."

"And I resent the fact that Chief Johnston's got me baby-sitting you to make sure you don't screw up again, at least not any more than you already have."

So the Chief does have my back. Well, that's good to know.

I knew that Finkle wanted me out, but he wasn't going to jeopardize his own position and his access to the police hierarchy just to get at me.

I took a deep breath, my arms still folded across my chest, and said, "You don't have to sweat it, Henry. I didn't know Overbeek was going to react the way he did. I'm going to write up all my notes and you'll have everything on your desk this afternoon. You can take it from there." I smiled, lifting my chin.

"You think you're pretty smart, don't you?" He snarled.

"I'm sure I don't know what you're talking about, Henry." I pouted my lips.

"Just remember, Gazzara, every good cop has connections with the local government."

"Oh, I see. Every *good* cop. Got it." I thought about Cassandra Smart: I knew exactly how she felt.

"Stop looking for more toes to step on, Kate. I don't just do favors for the warm fuzzies. One of these days I'll expect you to return the favor." He licked his lips and I nearly shot out of my seat to slap him across the face. But I held onto myself.

"Maybe we should discuss this with Chief Johnston." I never wanted to take that route. I never wanted to threaten Finkle like that, but he was pushing my buttons. Intentionally.

"Just remember who you have to answer to, Kate." He leaned back.

Just then there was a knock on my door. A plump woman in a suit smiled at me and waved.

"Sorry to interrupt," she said cheerfully.

"I'm just leaving, Betty. She's all yours," Finkle said without looking at me as he left.

"Lieutenant Catherine Gazzara?" Betty stepped into my office.

"Yes, ma'am."

"Hi. I'm Detective Betty Lake with Internal Affairs." She was just as pleasant as could be. Had I not known what she was there for I'd have thought she was a kindergarten teacher or maybe a greeter at the Walmart.

"Detective Lake." I stood and extended my hand, but I couldn't bring myself to smile at her.

"I just need to borrow a couple of your files." She handed me a small post-it with two familiar names on them. One was a bust I'd made of a guy who was selling junk under a bridge. The other was for his associate who'd robbed a chain of liquor stores. I pulled them from underneath a stack and hoped they'd be up to snuff.

"Thank you so much. I'll return them before you even realize they're gone."

"Take your time," I said, unable to hide the snark in my voice. "Those guys aren't going anywhere."

She shrugged and smiled as she left my office. I scooped up Cassandra's file and a couple of others that needed my attention and decided to call it a day. I was sure Finkle wouldn't be looking for me any further. The Chief had already yelled at me once this week so I figured I was good for at least a couple more days. I patted Lonnie on the shoulder as I walked past his cubicle.

"Where are you headed?"

"Home," I said. "I need to clear my head."

"IA give you a hard time?" He looked at me like a dog waiting to get his ears scratched.

"That Detective Lake is one deceptive... She's like somebody's grandma." I wrinkled my nose.

"That's not too bad." Lonnie shrugged.

"Are you kidding? I'm going to have nightmares about it for weeks. At least if the person looked like Nosferatu, they'd fit the image of Internal Affairs. Sending a pudgy Oompa Loompa just messes with your head."

Lonnie's laugh shook his entire desk. I told him I'd call him if I needed anything and he promised to do the same if he heard anything about my situation being batted around the bullpen. But I wasn't going to hold my breath. Finkle would make darn sure that anything that had to do with the investigation into my behavior would be kept under wraps until he said so. I was sure he'd want a front-row seat.

If I could just get Cassandra Smart's case a little

closer to being closed, I'd be happy... Well, not really, but you know what I mean, right?

By the time I made it home it was just after five. I'd had to make a few stops along the way. I needed stamps and a trip to the post office on Shallowford Road was never quick. Talk about a cushy job. Twelve people were in line. There were three windows, but only one person working while the others traded jokes in the back.

When I got out of there, I realized I was hungry, so I decided it was a perfect night for a bucket of fried chicken to go. I also remembered I was down to my last few drops of wine, and that meant a stop at the liquor store was in order. That done I went home, ate more of the chicken than I should have, along with a large glass of red, and then I took a nap. I woke an hour later to my phone ringing. It was Lonnie.

"Hey, Lonnie," I said, still half asleep, "what's up?"

"You need to come on in. Kyle Hendrick is here and is demanding to talk to you."

13

I don't want to tell you how many red lights I squeaked past in my haste to get to the PD. I left my car parked on a diagonal between the two yellow lines on the lot and sprinted to the front door when I saw Lonnie standing there holding it open for me.

"What's he said?" I panted.

"Nothing yet, except that he wants to talk to you, but he's ready for a fight, Kate. I put him in Interview Room B. I didn't think your office was a good idea."

"Thanks," I muttered as I walked toward the hallway that led to the three interview rooms. I stood for a minute in the observation room, watching him through the one-way window. Kyle Hendrick was standing with his hands on his hips, staring down at a blank legal pad on the table, muttering to himself.

"You're right," I said. "He's pissed. I wonder what that's about? Well, I'd better go talk to him. You stay here. Turn the cameras on. Take notes, if you want."

As I walked into the interview room I said, "Good

evening, Mr. Hendrick." He turned to face me. He was angry. "I should warn you before you say anything that this interview is being recorded. Now, what can I do for you?"

"I can't believe you came to my office this morning. Do you have any idea how much trouble you caused me?" He wasn't exactly shouting but he was as close to it as a person could get.

I closed the door.

"I'm sorry Mr. Hendrick. It wasn't my intention to cause problems for you, but I'm conducting a murder investigation and—"

"Yeah. A murder that took place a hundred years ago. Who the hell cares? It's over and done with. Why can't you just leave it alone?"

"You're kidding me, right?" I put my hands on my hips, showcasing the badge on my belt as well as my weapon. *Damn, I should have left that outside.*

"I don't want you mentioning my name regarding this case anymore. You understand?" He shook his head but looked down at the table as he spoke. "And leave Tim Overbeek out of it, too."

"I'm sorry, Mr. Hendrick, but I don't answer to you. You can't come in here and tell me how to run my investigation. That isn't how this works... Tim Overbeek? Why are you worried about him? Has he called you? Warned you off?"

He groaned and ran his hands through his hair, pulling it even further off his forehead. He paced toward the mirror window then turned and faced me.

His eyes looked all over the room, down at the floor,

to the door, and finally at me. I couldn't tell if he was going to cry or if they were full of rage. Either way, this man was suffering, and I needed to talk him off the ledge.

"Kyle, something has obviously upset you. Why don't we sit down and talk it through?" I said softly but firmly. Being compassionate and patient wasn't exactly my strongest suit but, thankfully, he did as I asked. He jerked the chair out from under the table and flopped down on it.

"You don't understand," he said. "My boss saw you guys at the showroom. He's been asking all kinds of questions, questions I couldn't answer: Is there anything he needs to know? Have I screwed one of the customers? Will you be back? Does it have to do with the car lot? I don't want to lose my job, okay?"

I nodded. "I understand, and I know it's difficult, Mr. Hendrick. But if you are holding something back that has to do with this case, and I find out about it, it will definitely have a negative impact on your job." I paused. "It'll also have a negative impact on your future. Obviously, it has already."

"No! That's not true! I'm not holding anything back." He slammed his hand on the table. "Everything was fine until you started asking questions! I'd forgotten about the dumpster. I'd forgotten about those bad days. I'd moved on with my life. Yes, Tim Overbeek called me yesterday. He's totally pissed, told me that I better, and I quote, 'keep my damn mouth shut.'"

Did he now? I thought. *That's interesting.*

"It was over and done with," he said. "Now it's all

going to be back in the media! That night, the dumpster, everything. How can you destroy people's lives like this?"

"I think you have things backwards, Kyle." I slowly sat down across from him. "Cassandra Smart was murdered, remember? Her killer hasn't been caught. It's my job to catch him. Do you really think he should be allowed to get away with it, with destroying *her* life?"

Kyle's bottom lip trembled as he clenched his teeth. He was coming apart. There was something he was hiding. The dumpster incident... What Tim Overbeek did to Kyle had obviously terrified him, traumatized him even into adulthood.

"Other than that call he made, have you talked to Tim Overbeek?" I asked, watching his eyes... and there was the tell, a slight twitch of his left eyelid.

"No! I haven't," he lied.

"I've got an idea, Kyle," I said. "Here, take this." I slid the blank pad toward him and handed him a pen.

"What do you want? A confession?" He snorted.

"Do you want to make a confession?" I asked, looking hard at him.

"Hell no. I've nothing to confess to."

"I didn't think so," I said. "No, that's not what I was getting at, Kyle, but sometimes, when you write them down, it's easier to sort things out. I do it all the time. It helps; it really does. Why don't you give it a try? Write down your concerns, or just whatever comes to mind." I took a deep breath. "I'll go get you a bottle of water. Okay?"

He looked at the pad of paper and picked up the pen,

paying no attention to me as I stepped out into the corridor.

"He's covering for him," Lonnie said when I entered the observation room.

"Overbeek? You think?"

"Yeah, I do."

For several minutes, we watched Hendrick through the one-way window. He sat hunched over the pad but he wasn't writing.

"Maybe he *is* covering for him," I said, thoughtfully. "Maybe he's recovering regressed memories. My God, can you imagine, four hours inside that dumpster? The temperature in that thing must have been... over a hundred, and the stink of the rotting garbage? I can't even imagine what this guy's been carrying around with him all these years. Yeah, I'd say he's badly traumatized. Overbeek should have gone to jail for that."

"Do you think he's going to write anything down about what Overbeek did?"

"I don't know, Lonnie. To be honest, I can't even tell if he's writing or if it's just his hand shaking."

I unfolded my arms. "I'm going to go get him a water. Maybe he'll open up a little more."

When I stepped back into the interview room, I couldn't help but notice the look on Kyle's face. His eyes were darting wildly back and forth. His lips were clamped tightly together and he was on his feet, standing in front of the table as if he'd kicked the chair out from behind him. The pad was blank, or so I thought. He wasn't planning on telling me anything.

"Mr. Hendrick, how about a water?" I held one of the

two bottles I had in my hand out for him. He slapped it away.

"This is intimidation!" he shouted.

Oh hell. All I need is for sweet-faced Betty Lake to hear this and come running to investigate.

"Kyle, please calm down."

"I will not calm down! I'm being held here against my will!"

Was I ever glad the cameras were running?

"That's not true, Kyle. You came here of your own volition, remember? You asked to talk to me. You're free to go whenever you like." I pointed to the door and shifted from my right foot to my left.

He stopped panting, holding his breath for a second as he realized that I was right. He seemed to calm down a little.

"Great! I'm outa here."

"Of course, Kyle. There's the door. I'll show you out of the building... One thing though: you should know before you go, that until you tell us what we need to know, about Tim Overbeek and his connection to Cassandra Smart's murder, we *will* be talking to you again."

Before I knew it Kyle was rushing around the table at me. But, like a well-trained rottweiler, Lonnie stepped into the room.

Hendrick stopped dead in his tracks. He would have been in trouble if he'd tangled with me. I can more than hold my own in a scrap, but Lonnie would have taken him apart, and he knew it.

"Fine. Then I'm leaving, now. And you'd better leave

me the hell alone from now on. If you bother me again, I'll file harassment charges against you. And that won't be all." His bottom lip trembled again.

"What did you say?" I asked.

"Are you threatening a police officer?" Lonnie tilted his head to the left, looking him in the eye.

"You take it any way you want. But I know all about you, Lieutenant, and I will not be the victim of police brutality." He plowed his shoulder into Lonnie's arm as he pushed past us and out of the room.

I looked at my watch, then said, "Interview concluded by the interviewee at eight-thirty-three."

Then I picked up the pad and Lonnie followed me to the observation room and I stopped the cameras.

"What the hell?" I looked up at Lonnie. "Okay, you saw the whole thing. I didn't lay a finger on him."

"I thought you exercised amazing strength and restraint. I wanted to reach through the glass and shake his ass." Lonnie sniffled.

"Uh-oh. Are you catching my cold?" I took a deep breath through my nose and was happy to realize I was breathing freely again.

"Oh hell, I hope not." He rubbed the back of his neck. "I'm feeling okay... I think."

"You think? I think you should do yourself a favor. Go home. Take a hot shower and down a couple gallons of vitamin C. Don't do what I did and just pretend it isn't happening." I glanced at the notepad, and I couldn't help but smile. He had written something after all, just three little words: "Go f— yourselves."

"Nice," I said, holding it up for Lonnie to see.

"Yeah, nice. But who will he call when he gets robbed? Us, and he'll want us there immediately."

Lonnie took the pad from me and tore out the sheet, crumpled it up and tossed it into the trash can.

"Yeah well," I said, regretfully, "that's the way it is these days. Learned his manners the same place Tim Overbeek did, I guess. What a pair of asses... So Overbeek called him... I wonder what that was about, other than to tell him to keep his mouth shut? You saw him lie, right?"

He nodded. "Sure did."

I took a deep breath. "Go home, Lonnie. I'm going to go talk to Finkle about this."

"Are you sure?"

"Oh yeah. I don't' want to, but I have to. I'm not supposed to contact Overbeek, not without Finkle's permission, but he's got Hendrick so terrified he's resorting to threatening police officers, and I'd really like to know what he, Finkle, plans to do about it. Not to mention that I need to cover my own ass, right?"

Lonnie grinned. "I hear ya. Good luck, LT. See you tomorrow."

I went to the first floor where Finkle's office was, half hoping his door would be locked up tight with the lights off. But, no such luck. The door was cracked open and the soft glow from his desk lamp gave his office an almost romantic hue. I couldn't help but feel slightly grossed out as I approached the door and knocked.

"Hey, you got a minute?"

"To what do I owe this unexpected pleasure?" He smirked.

I cleared my throat and said,"I wanted to talk to you about the Cassandra Smart case."

"I took a look at that this afternoon. Strange case. And what a waste. I'd have let her eat crackers in my bed any time." He leaned back in his leather, high-backed chair and waited for my response.

As quickly and as accurately as I could I told him what happened with Kyle Hendrick. I also made sure to let him know that Lonnie had been there with me the entire time and that the interview had been recorded.

"Lonnie Guest," he said. It came out like he had a nasty taste in his mouth.

Finkle and Lonnie had a love/hate relationship. They loved to hate each other.

"Can you believe that guy?" he asked. "What's with him? So he lost a few pounds—so what? He's still a dumb son of a bitch and always will be."

I didn't answer. I couldn't, not without getting myself into more trouble. Truth be told, I wanted to reach right across the desk and bitch-slap him. But instead I gifted him with a look I hoped would turn him to stone. Oh, if only...

"So, you think this guy Hendrick is covering for Tim Overbeek?"

"I do. He's definitely covering something. I thought that maybe he was still traumatized by what Overbeek had done to him. You know he tossed him in a dumpster and almost killed him, right?"

He nodded, so I continued, "Kyle Hendrick was locked inside that steel box in the dark, in the heat of the night for more than four hours. According to the file he pissed himself, lost control of his bowels, and threw up. He was barely conscious, because of the heat, not to mention the stink, when they dragged him out. He was up to his waist in... well... waste. He filed a complaint but then for some reason called it quits. I think someone got to him; probably Overbeek Senior. Anyway, I don't think he ever got over it, or forgave Tim Overbeek."

I waited for Finkle to make a smart remark, but he didn't. He just sat there, his fingers steepled and pressed to his lips.

"The dumpster incident was just a few days before Cassandra's body was found," I continued. "I'm convinced that Hendrick knows something about the night she was killed and that he's covering it up. I think he knows Overbeek killed her, probably in a drunken rage... Henry, why would Hendrick, humiliated as he was, file charges and then drop them the next day? It makes no sense. I tried to get him to talk, but I couldn't get through to him."

"You mean your torture techniques had no effect on him?" Finkle smirked.

"Oh come on, Henry. I've never tortured anyone and you know it."

"Maybe you should have tried sweet-talking him, opened another button, flashed a little skin. You know you'd get a lot further with honey than with vinegar. A lot further." He scooted his chair back a little and clasped his hands behind his head.

"Flashed a little skin?" I couldn't believe he'd said it. "Okay, Henry, if that's your suggestion, I'll take it under consideration." I stood up to leave.

"Now hold on, Gazzara. Lighten up a little. You take everything so personally." He chuckled as if it was all a funny joke that had gone over my head. "Okay, I'll handle the case from here on."

"What?"

"Put everything on my desk tomorrow morning and I'll take care of it." He scooted his chair closer to his desk and grabbed a fancy black pen from the gold-plated holder that was positioned right behind the plaque that read Henry Finkle Assistant Chief.

"Well, what are you going to do?" I asked.

"Are you questioning my authority, Lieutenant?"

"What? No. I'm just asking how you plan on proceeding."

"I plan on proceeding by the book; something you might try doing in the future. Good night, Lieutenant."

I didn't try to hide my disappointment. Right then I realized I'd made a big mistake unloading on Finkle, and damn it, I should have known better. If I'd kept my mouth shut, I could maybe have squeezed in another couple of days before I was forced to hand it over.

I rose from my seat, nodded at him, went back to my own office and scooped up the file from my desk. Oh how I wanted to go throw it at Finkle's head. I stood for a minute, considering my options.

"He said in the morning," I muttered to myself. "Okay then. Tomorrow it is."

In truth, I felt like I wasn't done with it, that I still had a little time left. So I tucked the file under my arm and left the building. There had to be something I was missing.

As soon as I got home I locked the door, kicked off my shoes, pulled off my pants and poured myself a glass of wine. I took a quick sip. Too quick. I choked, gasped, and several red drops speckled the front of my best white blouse.

I groaned but left the blouse on. It was already ruined... and it wasn't like I had a date or anything.

I took another sip of wine. No, it wasn't a sip; it was a nice healthy gulp and I closed my eyes, savoring the taste.

I picked up the file, stood for a minute, eyes closed, glass in one hand, the file in the other, then I tossed it onto the coffee table, sat down on the couch, flipped it open, and picked up the first crime scene photo.

It was a horrible mess, the crime scene; one of the worst I'd seen. The poor girl had lived and suffered through almost all of the attack before death finally took her. And it had rained. She'd been left there, face down in all that muck and dirt.

I poured another glass of wine and looked at the photo like it was a "Where's Waldo" poster. I read Peete's notes and reread all the interviews.

This is nuts, I thought as I read through Tim Overbeek's interview. *He knew her in school. He wanted to date her. He was hardly a criminal mastermind since his father had to bail him out of one mess after another.* I looked at the pictures of the crime scene again. And suddenly wondered if I hadn't been barking up the wrong tree the entire time.

Overbeek's not that smart. In fact, he's a dumb ass... He would have gotten caught. Right away, like that same day.

I stared at the contents of the file until my eyes blurred. *What the hell am I missing.*

Finally, I gave it up and called it a night. Tomorrow I'd hand it all over to Finkle and watch as he not only got an arrest warrant but also an "atta-boy" from Internal Affairs.

Sleep didn't come easy that night. I tossed and turned and finally descended into an uneasy slumber filled with dreams, some of which bordered on nightmares: choppy, disjointed visions of Cassandra running, chased by a half-dozen shadowy, unrecognizable figures. Then I was running, beginning nowhere and ending... nowhere. I watched, unable to move as the figures pounced on her, stabbing... stabbing... stabbing... blood running in rivers in every direction. Faces grinning at me out of the shadows, none of them I recognized. Finkle handcuffing Cassandra... And then I woke up, fell out of bed and landed on my knees. I staggered to the bathroom, turned on the shower and stood there in the rain, the water scalding hot, my head down, both hands on the wall, barely able to think, my head was so full of crap.

I got out of the shower, wrapped myself in a towel and went to the window. It was still early. The sun was not yet up, but the sky was slowly pulling on that pale periwinkle robe. It would be crisp out there, exhilarating, a perfect morning for a run. And I knew just the spot.

South Chickamauga Creek was a twenty-five-minute drive from my apartment. Sure, I could have just headed off down the street in my neighborhood and gotten my cardio workout faster. But I needed to really clear my head. Plus, I'd be driving by a great coffee shop and I planned to reward myself with a large to-go cup on the way back.

The parking lot where the trails merged was empty except for a couple of other vehicles. One car had a bike rack and I assumed they were making use of the quiet time of morning to pedal around the Greenway. The other was a fairly new Honda Accord. I parked a few slots away from the other cars.

I locked my Glock 43 in the glove compartment, made sure my phone and badge were safely tucked inside my Spibelt along with a few other things a single woman jogging alone might find useful.

I closed the car door, locked it, took a few deep breaths, stretched my legs, pulled my arms over my head, did a couple of sideways stretches, then started out at a brisk walk. The path snaked its way along the line of trees for about half a mile before it turned into the deeper woodlands of the gorge. The temperature dropped a few more degrees once I was under the shade of the trees. The sounds of my feet clapping against the pavement and my breath coming harder and harder were loud in my ears. Above it all I could hear birds chirping their good mornings. The air was thick with moisture and smelled clean and new.

I finally reached the creek and followed the concrete path along side of it.

As I ran, the facets of the Cassandra Smart case spun through my head like a movie. I was on the same trail she would have taken had she been coming from a party at the university the night she was killed.

It was quite well-lit at nighttime since it joined the

outskirts of the campus with homes and apartments rented by the students. If Cassandra had been heading this way, she would have been traveling in the general direction of her home.

As I jogged and was beginning to feel the burn in my thighs, I wondered how much smaller the trees had been back in 1992 compared to how they looked now. The area where Cassandra's body had been found was a lush patch of reeds and tall grass that grew cattails and was home to frogs and lizards and mosquitos. According to the map that was in the file, I'd be coming up to that one-time crime scene in just a few more strides.

Once I was there, I was happy to stop. My mouth was dry and I could feel the sweat trickling down my back as I walked slowly to the spot where the body had been found.

I panted as I took in the entire area. But for a couple of telltale signs, it looked nothing like the pictures in the file. The tree where they'd found her purse had either grown out of recognition or it was gone.

The benches in the photos were also still in the same places although they'd received a fresh coat of paint sometime during the last couple of years.

Somehow, though, I knew exactly where it had happened, where she'd died. There was no memorial cross, no indication of what had happened there that night. I guess Cassandra didn't have anyone that cared enough to memorialize her: so sad.

"Come on, Cassandra, girl. Help me out here," I said to myself as I stood with my hands on my hips and looked around the scene. "What am I missing? What'll make Tim talk?"

I looked in the direction she'd have been coming from, and then I stepped a few paces in that direction. Overbeek would have had to have attacked her from behind. She had several wounds that indicated she had been stabbed in the back first. Then, when she fell, she either rolled over onto her back or he turned her over and continued his assault.

The wounds had been made by a left-handed assailant. I remembered that from Doc Sheddon's report. I thought back to when we visited Overbeek in his office. I remembered how pissed he was as we questioned him, and how he'd made notes, writing them down on a pad on his desk. It was a tactic I sometimes used to intimidate the interviewee, annoy them. I remember that it had annoyed me too when Overbeek... *Smart ass!* I thought, then, *Son of a... bitch.*

"Holy crap," I said out loud. "He wrote with his right hand." The sound of words out of my own mouth made me jump. "Tim Overbeek was writing with his right hand. I can see it as clear as day."

I paced for a minute and tried to remember exactly... Yes, I was sure it was his right hand. I was positive. Wasn't I?

I pulled my phone from my Spibelt and was about to dial Lonnie's number when I suddenly thought about Mark Smirin. *Did he write with his right or left hand? No, he didn't write at all... but he did hold his phone in his left hand.* I remembered that. *So for all intents and purposes, he's left-handed. What about Kyle Hendrick?*

Kyle Hendrick had written his little love letter to me with his right hand... I was sure he did. Or was I?

"No," I mumbled out loud. "He's a fickin' lefty. At the showroom he was writing with his left hand when we came in." I snapped my fingers. "I even said something about it. Yeah, I told Lonnie about lefties being geniuses."

I dialed Lonnie's number knowing he would probably still be sleeping; it wasn't even six-thirty in the morning yet.

"Hello?" he muttered sounding like he had a mouth full of marbles.

"Hey, I'm at the South Chickamauga Creek running trail. I have a question."

"Mom?"

"Don't be an ass. Tell me, Lonn—"

I didn't see it coming. There was a blinding white flash of light and the back of my head felt as if it had exploded. I felt my energy leave my body in a rush. My cell phone fell to the ground. There was a deafening ringing in my ears, and the pain... *Did a branch fall on me? Was I struck by lightening?*

I staggered a few steps forward and then collapsed to my knees... and then I heard the voice behind me.

"You frickin' bitch. You just couldn't leave it alone, could you? All these years and no one bothered about it. But you... you had to dig it all up again and... and..."

I knew that voice.

14

I crawled forward on my hands and knees, trying desperately to get away from him.

"She was a slut," Kyle Hendrick hissed. "She said she hadn't been with anyone but Mark, but we knew; we all knew. Everyone knew she was a slut."

I shook my head in an attempt to clear it, but all that did was make the ringing in my ears louder and the pain in my head even worse.

I twisted around and looked up at him; my eyes wouldn't focus, but Kyle's form was unmistakable. His waist was broader than his shoulders but not by much. He might not have had a washboard stomach but there was a hell of a lot of wallop behind that crack to the back of my head. My vision was blurred but I could see clear enough to know that it was him.

"Kyle, what the hell are you doing?" I managed to gasp.

His eyes glittered. "You, you stupid bitch. I'm gonna do you."

Oh geez, he's out of his mind. He's lost it.

"I got away with it once. I can do it again. Thanks to you, everyone thinks Tim killed Cassie. He can take the fall for this one too. What do I care?"

"Come on now, Kyle." I shook my head, cleared my throat. "Don't do this... What about your family?"

"Family." He charged me, grabbed me by the collar of my sweatshirt and jerked my face to within inches of his own. He smelled like he hadn't washed for days; his clothes were dirty, looked like they didn't fit. The jerky movement made my head swim. That was why everything looked so *off*.

"I don't have any family. I don't have a wife or a girl-friend. I have to pay for sex. I learned a long time ago that the only thing women care about is money. I knew all about Cassie. I even offered to pay her, but she was too good for my money."

"Kyle, you've got a problem," I said. "But it can be fixed. You can get help. You can." I barely recognized my own voice.

"Oh yeah, I have a problem, and you're it. You brought it all up again. You... you... You're not going to put me away, you bitch. Nobody's ever going to put me away again."

Shit! I knew he wasn't over that frickin' dumpster.

"It stops, right here, right now," he snarled as he reached behind him and pulled out a knife and held it up to my face.

My vision was blurry but—always the cop, even in a situation like that—I noted that it didn't have a guard and was sure it was the same blade used to kill Cassandra. And... yes, he was holding it in his left hand.

"This is my lucky blade." He smiled down at me.

"Lucky blade, my ass," I said. "It's going to put you away, Kyle. Now why don't you let me up and we go get a coffee and talk things over. I can help you—"

"What do you mean, 'it's going to put me away'?" he interrupted me. "No one knows about it. I kept it hidden."

I nodded. "That you did, Kyle. But there's no guard on it, and there was a lot of blood, wasn't there?"

He stared down at me but said nothing.

"Do you remember how your hand slipped off the handle as you kept on stabbing her? You cut your finger —*I sure as hell hope he did.* I sent her bag to the lab last week, to have it processed for blood. They're going to find it, aren't they, Kyle. Your blood; your DNA. On the bag... You're done, my friend. Why did you hang it up on that tree anyway? Why did you kill her?"

"I didn't mean to."

You didn't mean to? You stabbed her forty-four times for God's sake.

"I was on the Greenway when she came from the party. I told her hello. She ignored me, the bitch. I told her again. She ignored me again." He was talking like he was spaced out, eyes vacant, remembering.

"I grabbed her arm and she ran. I ran after her, caught her and she started screaming... She got away, ran, screaming. I caught her and... I... never... I never." He stopped talking.

I looked up at him. His face was white, his mouth hanging open, white stuff at the corners. He was holding my shirt with his right hand and the knife with his left hand. He had his hands full but there was no way I could pry myself out of his grip, so I managed to focus on what I could do. Get even closer... and with one awkward push I head-butted him, ramming the top of my head into his nose. He howled with pain but he didn't let go of my shirt or the blade. I twisted myself over sideways and kicked out with both feet and knocked the wind out of him. I struggled to pull away only to trip over my own feet and land flat on my back. Finally, my shirt tore and I was free, scooting away from him. If he were to get on top of me, it would be the end.

There was one more thing I carried with me every time I went for a run. I slid the Velcro bracelet from around my wrist to my hand while still madly kicking myself back and away from him. My back slammed into the trunk of a tree. I tried to inch my way to my feet but I couldn't; my head was spinning—everything was tilting from the blow to my head.

I felt like I was the only woman on the planet. There was no one around. Not another jogger, the person with the bike, or... the car. And then I remembered: *Oh my God! It has dealer plates. That was Kyle's car. Geez... I should have noticed them... but I didn't... Stupid, stupid, stupid... Stop it; you gotta get away from him.*

Kyle had stopped groaning and was staring at me with wild, wide eyes and flushed cheeks.

"You fricking bitch," he spat. "I'm gonna gut you like a freakin' fish."

"You came here to talk to her, didn't you, Kyle?" I said, desperately trying to buy a little time, feel the cool metal cylinder in my hand.

"Yeah, I came to talk to her; I came to tell her she was soon going to have company. And shit, was I ever right? You walked right into it. I heard you coming. Stupid bitch cop. You're so frickin' stupid. You think that badge makes you smart? Like Cassie? She thought that her blonde hair and her sexy body made her something special, that she was better than everyone else. But it didn't. She was noth-ing... nothing more than a piece of worthless trash."

"And you'd know all about trash, wouldn't you Kyle? You were up to your waist in it for several hours, like the nasty little rat you are."

He clenched his teeth.

"When they let you out of that dumpster you were humiliated, embarrassed, laughed at because you'd crapped and pissed yourself. You needed revenge. It was Overbeek that had locked you in the dumpster, but that was out of the question. He was too tough for you and he always traveled in a pack." I grimaced as I tried to focus on him.

"And besides, you knew his dad would make your life a living hell. So there you were raging inside, frustrated. So who then? Who was going to pay for what happened to you? Cassandra Smart. You made a play for her that night, didn't you? But she rejected you, humiliated you all over again. It was too much, so you killed her... All that rage came boiling out of you. Forty-four times you stabbed her. Did you know that, Kyle? Of course you didn't. You were out of your tiny mind with rage. And then, to top it all, you filed assault charges against Tim Overbeek. But Mayor Overbeek wasn't going to allow that. He paid you off. You were to drop the charges and never mention it again. Tim had beaten you again. You're one weak, pathetic wimp, Kyle."

He inched closer. The blade in his hand didn't scare me as much as the look in his eyes did. My head was splitting, spinning; my legs felt weak and I knew I was in trouble. So did Kyle.

Without warning he lunged at me, the blade glittered and flashed in the early morning sunlight. My reflexes kicked in. I jumped backward. The knife slid by over my left shoulder. The cylinder of pepper spray was tiny with a range of only four feet, but Kyle was a lot closer than that. I let him have it right in the eye. He staggered backward, screaming, his right eye shut tight, his left glaring at me. He turned and took off running, off the path and into the trees.

I heard someone shouting my name. At first I thought it was Kyle, but as I caught my breath and listened, I recognized the voice. It was Lonnie.

"Over here," I yelled, and sat down on the grass beside the path, and then he came running...

"How did you know?"

"Just relax, Kate. You're bleeding. What the hell happened? Where is he?"

"What? Calm down, Lonnie. What happened was Kyle Hendrick. He jumped me. I hit him with pepper spray. He took off into the trees that way."

When I pointed I saw what Lonnie had meant. The

sleeve of my sweatshirt was soaked with blood, all the way to my wrist and hand; so was the front, and even my pants. Oh yeah, I was bleeding.

"Oh shit, this looks bad," I said. I felt light-headed, dizzy. I reached up with my right hand, felt the goose egg on the back of my skull, and wondered if I was concussed. One thing I did know: it hurt like hell when I touched it.

Lonnie radioed in that we had a suspect loose on South Chickamauga Creek trail, and to send an ambulance and all available units. He also informed dispatch that Kyle Hendrick was to be considered armed and dangerous.

"Okay, let me see it," Lonnie said, and gently tore away the shirt where Kyle's knife had sliced through it.

"Oh shit, LT. He got you good. Take it easy. You're gonna need to go to the hospital."

"I think you are right, old buddy." I let out a pained breath, as he helped me to my feet and slid a beefy arm around my waist.

"Can you walk?"

"Yeah, I think so."

"Come on then. I'll help you."

And walk we did. The parking lot couldn't have been more than a quarter mile away, but it seemed like miles. By the time we got there, I was exhausted and still bleeding profusely. Fortunately, the ambulance had already arrived.

I remember very little of what happened next. I do remember the EMTs helping me into the back of the ambulance and lying me down on the gurney. I also remember one of them asking for my name and date of birth. After that, I remember nothing: I was in another place.

15

I t had been four days since I ran into Kyle Hendrick on the jogging path on South Chickamauga Creek. It turned out that I did indeed have a concussion, so I spent that night and the next day in Erlanger Hospital.

Chief Johnston visited me the following morning and ordered me to take a couple days off, and I was more than happy to oblige. Lonnie and several other colleagues also visited me. So did Harry and Tim. Henry Finkle? Hah, of course not.

The cut across the top of my shoulder was deep, to the bone, and required a dozen staples. It hurt like hell when I moved my arm.

Anyway, four days after the incident I was back at my desk talking to Lonnie and sipping on a huge mug of black coffee.

They didn't catch Kyle until late the following afternoon. An All-Points Bulletin had been put out for him along with the word that he'd injured a female officer so it was only a matter of time before they caught him.

"They found him at a rest stop in Georgia, on I-75 south of Tifton. He'd pulled in to sleep. He was in a car stolen from his own dealership, so it wasn't hard for the highway patrol to spot him."

"Let me guess. Heading for Florida?" I asked as I swiveled in my chair behind my desk. "Did he resist?" I asked, secretly hoping he had.

"Well, at first he denied who he was. It must have been quite a sight to see, but pathetic. There he was with five officers surrounding his vehicle, weapons drawn, demanding he get out of the car. You're not going to believe it, Kate. He wouldn't get out of the car because he'd pissed his pants. They had to drag him out. He insisted that they'd got the wrong man, that his name was Karl Hennessey and that his wallet had been stolen."

I shook my head. "Wow, you could almost feel sorry for him, if you didn't know what a wicked, crazy son of a bitch he is."

"You know you'll have to make a statement, right?" Lonnie said over the rim of his mug. "I'm... glad you're okay, Kate."

"Thanks. I'm glad you showed up when you did. If you hadn't..."

"Well, I heard most of it on the phone."

"What?"

"Yeah. Don't you remember? You called me?"

I didn't, not until that moment. "That's right. I did, didn't I? I remember now. I called you because Doc Sheddon had said the stab wounds had been inflicted by a lefty. Did you know that only ten percent of the population is left-handed, Lonnie?"

"I do now."

"Yeah, well, I saw Kyle writing in his office with his left hand. Remember? And do you remember I even made that comment about geniuses, that they were often lefties? Hah, he sure as hell is no genius."

Lonnie pinched his eyebrows together. "But when he was here, in the interrogation room, he wrote with his right hand. I saw him do it."

"Me, too. Here's another fun fact for you. Only one percent of the population is ambidextrous. Kyle Hendrick must be a one-percenter." I cradled my cup in both hands, leaned back in my chair, and took a sip of coffee.

"That's what I was calling you about," I said. "I wanted to see if you remembered if Mark Smirin was left or right handed. Turns out we didn't need to know. Kyle admitted to everything."

I set my coffee on the desk and folded my arms feeling very happy about the way this one ended.

"Well, I hate to do this to you, Kate, but I heard some gossip I think you should know about." He leaned forward to speak quietly and I did too, but before he could say anything the door opened and Henry Finkle walked in.

"Geez, Henry," I snapped. "Don't you ever bother to knock?"

"Chief Johnston wants you in his office pronto," Finkle snapped, and before I could answer he was gone.

I looked at Lonnie. His eyes were wide and he was on the edge of his seat.

"Don't bother to tell me, Lonnie. Looks like I'm about to find out for myself."

"Yeah, I guess. Good luck, Kate," he said, standing and letting me leave the office first.

When I stepped into Chief Johnston's office, I braced myself for the worst. Not only was he standing at his desk but Finkle was there in his usual spot looking serious as a tombstone. Cathy was also there sitting beside Finkle.

"Chief?"

"Close the door, Lieutenant, and have a seat."

Here it comes. Save me a place in the unemployment line.

"Internal Affairs has concluded their investigation," he said as he sat down.

I watched out of the corner of my eye as Cathy took shorthand notes.

"Although you were cleared of the more serious allegations of brutality, you were found to have used poor judgment and verbal intimidation in order to get the suspect to comply."

"You bet I used verbal intimidation," I snapped.

"Kate," he said, holding up a hand. "I'm trying to explain this to you. But if you're just going to sit there and make smart remarks, I'm afraid this will be but one of many discussions we'll be having about your behavior."

"No, sir. That's not it." I sighed and looked down at my shoes. "Were they not told about the Cassandra Smart case? That I wrapped up a twenty-three-year-old cold one? Don't I get any credit for that?"

"No. You don't. That file was supposed to have been handed over to Assistant Chief Finkle. As far as Internal Affairs is concerned it wasn't your case."

Of course it wasn't.

I didn't dare open my mouth or look in Finkle's direction.

"Lieutenant Gazzara, it was the opinion of IA that you should be punished with a week's suspension without pay."

My jaw hit the floor. "You've gotta be kidding me."

He ignored me and continued, "However, I informed them that the week's suspension would be sufficient, and that deducting your pay would be overkill. We were able to agree on that. Your suspension is effective immediately. Please hand over your badge and weapon."

I stood up, gently placed my badge and gun on the Chief's desk, and then stood and stared at him. For the first time in my life I felt hate in my heart. I now knew exactly why Harry had left the force. I also felt naked, and I knew that Finkle was enjoying my every uncomfortable minute. I turned my head and glanced at him and was surprised to see that he wasn't gloating after all.

"Use the week to get some rest, Kate," Johnston said, gently. "You need it; you've earned it."

"Yes, sir."

He turned his head and looked pointedly at Finkle and then back at me, and said, "You're a fine officer, Lieutenant. That's my considered opinion. Screw what IA thinks. That will be all. You can go now. Report to me when you return to work."

I went back to my office, grabbed my coffee and my

purse and left immediately. I didn't even stop to say goodbye to Lonnie. I could feel all eyes on me but I didn't care.

As soon as I got home, I kicked off my shoes and poured myself a glass of wine to help dull the thudding in my shoulder. I sat down and could have flipped on the television but I didn't. Instead, I grabbed an old tissue I'd left on my coffee table from when I was sick and wiped my eyes with it.

This time, though, I wasn't sick. This time, for the first time since I was ten years old, I was crying.

Two DAYS later there was a knock at my front door. I thought it was Harry. I hoped it was Harry. It wasn't. I opened the door to find Chief Johnston standing there, in full uniform, cap in hand. My heart sank. I looked like shit: bare feet, hair hanging loose, no makeup, and dressed in sweats.

"Oh hell, Chief, what have I done now?"

He smiled, something he rarely ever did.

"Can I come in for a minute?"

I shrugged. "Sure." I opened the door wide and stood back for him to enter. I never realized how big he was; he just about filled the opening.

"You want some coffee?" I said, hoping he didn't. He did, wouldn't you know it?

I slapped a K-cup into the machine then handed him the cup and made a second one for me.

"So, are you here to fire me, or what?" I asked.

"Nothing like that, Kate. I came by to see how you were doing. That's all."

Yeah, right, I thought.

"I'm fine," I said.

He sat quietly, thinking, sipping his coffee, staring at the tabletop. *What the hell?*

"Well," he said finally, "that wasn't all I wanted."

Oh shit, I thought. *Here it comes.*

"Go on," I said, lifting my cup to my mouth and staring at him over the rim.

"Kate," he lowered his cup and put it down. "I wanted you to know that I didn't agree with what happened to you. In fact, I was pretty upset about it..." He paused, thought for a moment, then continued, "I was able to save your pay, as you know, but I couldn't expunge IA's report. So, in order to lighten the blow, if that's possible, I've placed a note in your personnel file stating my own findings and that I strongly disagree with IA's."

I have to admit, I was touched.

"Kate," he reached across the table and placed his hand on top of mine.

Oh boy, this is really weird.

"You're one of the best officers, best detectives I have, but I have to be careful not to show favoritism, especially in front of Henry and, to some extent, Cathy. That places an extra burden on your shoulders, I know. Kate, I would hate to lose you, and that's really why I'm here."

I didn't know what to say, so I didn't say anything.

He took his hand away, and said, "I know Harry Starke wants you to work for him. Please, don't do it. It would be a huge mistake..." He saw the look on my face.

"No, no, please, don't get the wrong idea. I like Harry and he's also the best at what he does, but..."

You do? I thought. *He is? Pity you never let him know when he worked for you.*

"Yes," he continued, "you'd probably make more money working for him but, Kate. You're a cop at heart; you always will be. So, please tell me you'll be back at work on Monday."

I almost burst out laughing. Of course I'd be back to work on Monday. I never for a minute considered not being, but I wasn't going to tell him that.

"Yes, Chief. I'll be there on Monday, just like always."

Where else would I be? I thought. *As you said, I'm a cop. It's what I do; it's what I am.*

The End

THANK you for taking the time to read Cassandra. If you enjoyed it, you might like to read the following sample from Book 3 in the series, Saffron.

16

SAFFRON

A LT. KATE GAZZARA NOVEL BOOK 3

I t was one of those godforsaken nights made even worse by the mantle of rain-sodden mist that swirled within the confines of the narrow alley. The glow of a single streetlight at the entrance to what was optimistically called Prospect Street reflected off the watery surface of the blackened and blistered asphalt and speared the darkness like a glittering finger pointing at something lying on the ground beside the dumpster. What it was T.J. Bron couldn't identify. Not that he tried. Not that he was even interested. He was hungry, had been for as long as he could remember. He was also broke, soaked to the skin, miserable almost to the point of intolerance and wondering if perhaps the time might finally have come when he should end it all.

At that point, he was simply looking for a dry spot to contemplate the method of his own proposed demise. And it was also at that moment when he was blinded by the headlights of a car that appeared out of nowhere and headed toward him at high speed which, considering the confines of the narrow street, and that he couldn't see, alarmed him—no, it scared the shit out him. He flattened himself against the sodden brick wall and the car flashed by, throwing up a wall of water on either side. The driver's side of the car missed him by inches; the wall of icy water did not. For a moment he just stood there, dripping, watching the tail lights until, with a screech of the tires, they made a left turn and disappeared.

He let himself slide down the wall until his backside hit the wet asphalt, and there he sat; cold, wet, and more alone than he'd ever been.

Shit, even Nam was better'n this.

He drew his knees in, wrapped his arms around them, and let his head fall onto them. He was done, had enough. It was time. The only questions that remained were where and how.

He lifted his head, glanced to the left, shook it, then turned to look to the right. The dumpster looked promising. Well, not really, but beggars... *Yeah, that's what I am, a damned beggar. Well, no more.* He felt inside the pocket of the sodden U.S. Army Shell Parka. It was still there, though he wondered if he had the strength in his fingers to open the blade. *Okay, that's the how. A couple of quick slashes—it's cold. Shouldn't feel a thing—an' I'll bleed out in just minutes... yeah! Well, maybe later. Now, let's go take a look at the dumpster.*

He struggled to his feet and shuffled through the darkness and the rain toward what he figured to be his final resting place. *A friggin' dumpster... Hmm, about what I deserve, I suppose.* But as he approached the dumpster the spear point of light from the distant streetlamp again drew his attention to the unidentifiable black bulk lying at its far end. As he drew closer, he saw it was just one of a dozen or so black, plastic garbage bags stacked against the steel sides, or was it? Something about it looked familiar, but... *Ah, who gives a shit?*

Had he been interested enough to take a look, he might have figured it out, but he wasn't. He was tired, soaked to the skin, and wanted nothing more than a dry spot to settle down and—he fingered the pocket knife through the material—*Peace at last, oh Lordy, peace at last.*

Some of the bags were broken open, their contents spewing out onto the street. He stirred them with his foot, wrinkled his nose at the foul smell. *Rotten cabbage? Yeah, that and a whole mess of other putrid crap. No, not here. I ain't much, but I do deserve a little more than to go out with the trash.*

He stirred some more, hoping he might find an edible morsel, but all he found was more rotten food, vegetables and other disgusting, stinking messes dumped by the cooks from the back of the Chinese restaurant across the alley.

He shook his head, dejected, and pulled the hood of the heavy parka tighter over the ancient John Deere ball cap. He pulled down on the bill of the cap so that it covered his eyes and face, protecting them from the pouring rain and then, head down, arms folded across his chest, he shuffled around the end of the dumpster to the tiny open porch at the rear of the Sorbonne, so-called night club and haunt of the deplorables... and sometimes the slumming, smart set of Chattanooga.

He stepped inside, set his back against the steel door and slid down to sit on his haunches in the relative shelter of the porch, let his chin fall to his chest, and closed his eyes. For fifteen, maybe twenty minutes, he simply sat there, half-asleep, thinking, dreaming... remembering. Finally, he sighed, lifted his head, opened his eyes and peered around. He blinked as his eyes adjusted to the darkness of the shadow cast by the dumpster. At first, he could see almost nothing, only the single finger of light from the distant streetlamp that fell upon...

What the hell is *that?* He wondered.

With an effort, he grabbed the steel doorknob, heaved himself upright, and then walked unsteadily to the dumpster. With one hand on the steel side, he steadied himself, leaned down and grabbed the corner of the black plastic wrapping and pulled. The rain-soaked painter's tape gave way, the plastic peeled back, and a pair of dead eyes stared up at him.

"*Oh shit!*" He dropped the edge of the plastic sheet back in place, staggered backward into the porch, then turned and hammered on the steel door with both fists, yelling obscenities. And he kept on hammering until finally the door screeched open a couple of inches and two bleary eyes glared at him through the gap.

"What the hell you doin', T.J.?" Benny Hinkle yelled at him. "It's past three. Get your ass outta here before I kicks it all the way to the damn river." He pushed the door to close it, but T.J. rammed it with his shoulder, knocking Benny backwards into the dimly lit passageway.

"There's a body out there, you fat asshole. I ain't got no phone. Call the damn police, for Chrissake!"

"Body? What body? Lemme see." He rushed out into the rain, to where T.J. was pointing.

"Holy crap," Benny said, as he lifted the corner of the plastic sheet. "I know her. Get your ass in here while I make the call."

"Screw you. I'm outta here." And T.J. turned, but before he could take a step, Benny grabbed him by the arm and hauled him in through the door. Any other time, T.J., an ex-Vietnam vet, would have been too much for him. As it was, T.J. was in bad shape and Benny had little trouble steering him down the passageway and into the empty bar.

He picked up two glasses and a bottle, slammed them down on the bar top, and said, "You pour while I make the call."

Ten minutes later, Prospect Street was ablaze with flashing blue and red lights.

17

CHAPTER 2

I was in bed when the call came in. The jangling tone and incessant buzzing of my iPhone dragged me back into the land of the living. I raised myself up on my elbows and stared through my hair at the bedside clock and groaned; it was just after four. I'd been in bed for less than three hours, having spent the hours between eleven and one in the morning following up on a drive-by shooting in East Lake.

I ran my fingers through my hair, pushed it back away from my eyes, and made a wild grab for the phone. I squinted at the display. *Damn!*

I rolled onto my side and tapped the screen. "This better be good, Lonnie," I growled.

"Yeah. I figured as much. Sorry LT. We've got a new one. In the alley behind Benny Hinkle's place. I'm on my way there now."

I flopped back down on the pillows, the phone still at my ear, "Okay. I'll be there as quick as I can." And I hung up before he had a chance to respond.

I dragged myself out of bed, staggered to the window, and stared out. It was raining; the water was coursing down the pane in rivulets. *Damn, damn, damn.*

I took two steps back, sat down on the edge of the bed, put my head in my hands, and wished to die. I sat like that for several moments, then dropped my hands to my knees, shook my head, and rose unsteadily to my feet.

Okay Kate, I thought. *Shower and coffee and you'll feel better.*

Thankfully, I'd set the coffee machine before I went to bed. All I had to do was push the button, and then head for the shower.

It was cold in my apartment. I'd lowered the heat before hitting the sheets. No matter, I turned the shower on cold, took a deep breath, and stepped in. The shock of the icy water would have killed a penguin. I wasn't in there more than ten seconds before I literally leapt out and grabbed a towel. I hurriedly toweled off, my teeth clattering like castanets, my skin a half-acre of goose-bumps. I dropped the towel on the floor and headed, naked, for the kitchen. I poured a mug of steaming black coffee, sat down, cradled the cup in both hands, and sipped, relishing the sensation of the scalding, bitter liquid as it coursed down my throat and through my chest.

Any other time, I would've sat and enjoyed the coffee, but I had no time for that. I dressed quickly in jeans, shirt, sweater, and rubber boots. I clipped my holster and badge to my belt, swallowed another quick slug of coffee, slipped into my old Barbour jacket—the damn thing was still wet—grabbed my keys and an already soggy umbrella, and hightailed it out the door.

By the time I arrived at the entrance to Prospect Street, the heavy overnight rain had diminished to a fine drizzle; better, but still cold and uncomfortable.

I parked on the adjoining street, close to the entrance to Prospect, and trudged through the rain, head down, umbrella up, toward the lights and the familiar white canvas tent erected over the body. My partner Lonnie Guest was already there, so were Doc Sheddon, Mike Willis, and at least a dozen uniforms. Even dressed in wet-weather clothing, they looked like a pack of half-drowned rats.

Lonnie held up the tape as I ducked under.

"Welcome to hell," Mike Willis said as we joined them. He moved in close, under the umbrella.

"Yes, you can say that again," I responded, leaning away from him a little; he didn't seem to notice.

"Welcome to..." He caught the look I shot at him and didn't finish. Instead he grinned at me, shrugged, and twitched his head in the direction of the tent, now just a couple of feet away.

"There's not much room in there," he said. "Doc's inside. I'll let him know you're here."

He stepped away and pulled back the flap, "Hey, Doc. Lieutenant Gazzara is here."

"Send her on in."

Willis stepped back and held the flap for me. I handed the umbrella to him and ducked inside.

Doc was crouched down beside the naked body of a young woman. I crouched down beside him. She appeared to be in her mid-twenties. She was lying on her back—legs straight, knees and feet together, arms by her sides—on a large sheet of black polythene, in which she had obviously been wrapped. In the light of the four LED lamps, hung from the support bars of the canopy, her skin resembled the color of day-old oatmeal. Her eyes, wide open, were brown, at least they had been, having turned cloudy, almost white in death.

"Wrapped up in the polythene, she was," Doc said, in a voice that was a passable imitation of the inimitable Yoda. "And dumped, she was." We rose up together.

Doc Sheddon is Hamilton County's chief medical examiner. I say Chief, but there is only one medical examiner in Hamilton County: him. Doc's a small man, five-nine, overweight, almost totally bald, with a round face. The Yoda impression was, I think, his way of making light of what appeared to be an ugly situation. Not that he disrespects the dead, he doesn't. But after a lifetime of dealing with them, and speaking for them, he's grown a little jaded these last few years.

We stood together for a moment staring down at the body. Me with my arms folded, Doc with his hands clasped behind his back.

"Don't ask," he said, without looking up. "Not more than a few hours," he continued, answering my unasked question anyway. "Lividity is not quite set, so she's been lying on her back for two or three hours. I'd say she died between midnight and two o'clock this morning, no earlier, and then dumped here. One good thing, though, the plastic sheet kept her dry and slowed the cooling process. Maybe we'll get lucky and find some trace...

Age? Between eighteen and twenty-five, I should think."

"The cause?" I asked, knowing only too well what his answer would be. "I see ligature marks on her neck."

"Come on, Kate, you know I can't say for sure, not until I do the post, but you're right. She was probably strangled to death. Anyway, I can't do anything more here. I need to get her back to the lab, out of the weather. I'll do the post tomorrow morning if you want to attend."

"Do I have a choice? Yes," I said, without waiting for an answer. "I'll be there."

I backed out of the shelter leaving him alone with the body. Once again, he had his chin on his chest and was staring down at the corpse.

Outside, in the rain, which had again increased in intensity, Lonnie was talking to Mike Willis. I joined them and took possession of my umbrella.

Lieutenant Mike Willis is head of our CSI department, has been for more years than I can remember. He's a strange little man, not unlike Doc in appearance. He too, is short and overweight, but whereas Doc is always tidy and well dressed, Mike is a little... scruffy—clean, but untidy and always in a hurry—head shaved and oiled, eyebrows thick and bushy, and a pair of hands—huge— that a gorilla would have been proud of.

"So, Mike," I said. "What do you think?"

He rolled his eyes, looked up at the still-dark sky, into the falling rain, shook his head, and said, "I think it's a washout, literally. Look at it. The street's a river. Kind of reminds me of that opening scene from *IT*. All that's missing is Georgie, the paper sailboat, and the scary clown. I'll do what I can, but I doubt very much that we'll find anything out here. Whatever there is, it's either on the body or that plastic sheet. I can't work either of them, not in this mess, so we'll to have to wait until she's in the lab."

I nodded. I wasn't surprised to hear it; disappointed, but it was to be expected.

"Are you going to attend the postmortem tomorrow Mike?"

"Yeah, I need to go over the body with the light, before Doc starts cutting on it. Here he comes. Hey, Doc. What time tomorrow morning? I need to light her up before you get started."

Doc nodded. "I'd like to get started by ten. Can you be done by then?"

Mike shook his head, "I dunno. I'll do my best. If I can get started on it by eight-thirty..."

"That'll work," Doc said. "Right now, I need to go. Things to do, people to see, and a body in the refrigerator that needs my attention, but I need a word with the paramedics first." He looked at me then at Mike then at Lonnie and said, "I'll see y'all tomorrow morning." And then he left, waddling through the rain toward the flashing red lights of the ambulance, his big black bag swinging from his right hand.

"Mike," I turned to him. "You want to go get some breakfast?"

He shook his head, "I wish I could, but I can't. I gotta get back to the lab too." He looked around the scene, then continued, "I'll leave the crew here, though. Waste of time, I'm sure, but..." He shrugged, then said, "I'll see you later, maybe?"

"Yes, maybe," I said, watching as the paramedics carefully rewrapped the body in its plastic sheet. That done, they zipped it into a body bag and loaded it onto a gurney. By the time they'd finished and were wheeling her away, Mike had left.

I turned to Lonnie and said, "Come on. I need some hot food and coffee." I looked at my watch. "Damn it. It's not yet six o'clock..." It was then I suddenly realized that Lonnie was unusually quiet. *What the hell is wrong with him I wonder?*

"You okay Lonnie?"

"No, not really... I, I'm thinking this is getting old. I've seen enough death to last me a couple of lifetimes. I know now how Harry felt, why he got out, all those years ago. Doesn't it get old for you, too, Kate?" He didn't give me a chance to answer before continuing, "Did you notice how young she was, how... how beautiful? She was just a kid... just a kid."

Now that was a surprise. I'd always thought Lonnie was a hard-ass. He's an intimidating presence, there's no doubt about that.

"Excuse me. Are you going soft on me, Lonnie?"

He shrugged. "Nah, not so's you'd notice... well, maybe. I just can't help but feel... Ah, what the hell. Let's go get us a chicken biscuit, or two." And with that, he turned and walked away leaving me standing there staring after him. *Wow!*

·   ·   ·

THAT'S IT. If you liked it, you can grab the complete story here: My Book

And in the UK here:

MY BOOK

THANK YOU.

Thank you again for taking the time to read Cassandra, and the short sample of Saffron. If you enjoyed it, please consider telling your friends or posting a short review on Amazon (just a sentence will do). Word of mouth is an author's best friend and much appreciated. Thank you. Blair Howard.

Reviews are so very important. I don't have the backing of a major New York publisher. I can't afford to take out ads in the newspapers and on TV, but you can help get the word out.

To those many of my readers who have already posted reviews to this and my other novels, thank you for your past and continued support.

If you have comments or questions, you can contact me by email at blair@blairhoward.com, and you can visit my website http://www.blairhoward.com.

Made in the USA
Las Vegas, NV
19 February 2022

44230285R00105